SAM CRESCENT & STACEY ESPINO

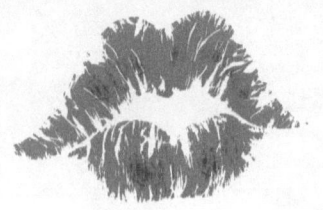

EVERNIGHT PUBLISHING ®

www.evernightpublishing.com

Copyright© 2017

Sam Crescent & Stacey Espino

Editor: Karyn White

Cover Artist: Jay Aheer

ISBN: 978-1-77339-283-7

ALL RIGHTS RESERVED

TAKING HER INNOCENCE

Killer of Kings, 1

Sam Crescent & Stacey Espino

Copyright © 2017

Chapter One

"You think you can handle it?" Boss asked.

Viper stared out across the parking lot. A lot of shoppers were milling around today, going about their own pathetic lives, believing they were the most important thing in the world.

None of them had any idea that one of the world's deadliest killers was amongst them. He was part of an elite group of mercenaries. He killed for the money. Whoever offered the highest bounty, he took it. He never asked questions, and he never cared about the people he killed. This was a job to him, something he was good at.

"Why can't I handle it? Send me a picture of the girl. I'll do the rest."

"She has to die of natural causes."

Viper snorted. "No problem."

He had one month to find a woman, and to end her life. Piece of cake. He had lots of ways of killing a woman, and this would be no different.

"Deposit the money, and I'll call you if I need more." Viper whistled as he made his way toward the car. He put the groceries in the trunk, got behind the wheel, and waited.

Her picture came through his cell phone, and he stared at the girl in question. She couldn't have been older than fifteen, but from what Boss had told him, she was nearly twenty-one years old, and had been on the run for nearly six months. *Curious.*

The picture showed her cuddled up next to her mother, and she looked happy. Pepper was chubby, her cheeks looking like the kind you could pinch, and grandmothers cooed over. Boss had given him all the details over the phone. Viper didn't do paperwork, reading, or worrying about something being tracked.

He memorized everything. All the little details were up in his head, and that was where they would stay until the job was gone.

Viper didn't know why the woman in question, Pepper, was running, and he really didn't care. The moment Boss called him and gave him an assignment, he did it. Now he just needed to figure out where she was staying.

Good news for him, he had a special guy who owned equipment that could find him this woman. Leaving the grocery store, Viper made his way across the city toward the guy who he knew would hook him up.

Whenever he was in between jobs, he would always stick around where his people were so that he didn't have to worry about endless traveling. Working for Killer of Kings was rather lucrative. They were a company known for getting the job done. Nothing was too much, no job too hard. He had traveled all over the world to do what needed to be done, from killing people, to fucking women, to even rescuing people. If the price was right, he would do anything.

From a young age, younger than any child should ever have to deal, he had been taught to hunt, to kill, and to do it without feeling a damn thing. There were scars on his back that all bled together that reminded him a past he wished he could forget. When he saw children with their parents, for a split second he felt envious, jealous that they could be having a wonderful life, a better one than he ever had. Of course they were having a better life than he had. None of them had ever gone through the hours of pain or the training that had made him one of the deadliest men on earth.

Parking his car outside of one of the shittiest apartments in the city, he made his way toward his contact, Maurice. The guy was thirty years old, a slob, but damn good when it came to computers. He was the only one who gave Viper the facts without giving him files thick with writing and shit. Viper didn't want to be studying. Cold, hard facts were what he was after, and he didn't need paperwork that could be traced.

Maurice lived on the top floor. He was a tall, skinny man who wore big, thick glasses. Banging on the door, Viper waited, and when Maurice opened the door his shirt was covered in ketchup and mustard stains.

"I've told you to change," Viper said, entering the room.

"Yeah, well, I didn't think I'd see you for a couple more weeks. You usually take time off. Why are you back after just a week?" Maurice asked.

The apartment was littered with debris. Only the sitting room, the place where all the computers and equipment were set up was spotless.

"You need to get a cleaning lady," Viper said. He hated mess.

Mess equaled mistakes.

He was clean, efficient, and he didn't have anything to leave behind. Even his apartment where he stayed during his vacations didn't hold any personal mementos. Not that he would ever have those. Mementos would mean caring, and that wasn't what he did. He didn't have a family, a past, nor would he have a future.

"Cleaning ladies touch stuff, and I know where everything is."

Viper looked around the apartment. "It stinks."

"So? It keeps everyone out, okay? This is my mess. My problem. Not yours. What do you want?" Maurice asked, shoving his glasses up his nose.

"Fine." Viper handed over his cell phone. "Get me everything on her."

"Do you have a name?" Maurice asked.

"Pepper. I want everything on the face though. You've got your computers that can track CCTV. I want to know where she was last seen."

"This could take a while."

"Don't care. I can pay." Viper moved into the sitting room and took a seat. It was the only place he was willing to park his ass while he waited, and there wasn't a chance in hell he was leaving until he got what he wanted.

Something was bugging him about this assignment, which was strange because he usually didn't care. Swift, efficient, done. That's what he'd always been about.

Maurice was humming as he got to work, scanning her picture, and then tracking it through the database. On the big screen in front of them, he saw several names and pictures as it did the recognition thing.

The beauty about security and live feeds everywhere was anyone could be tracked or traced. Unless someone knew how to avoid the cameras and the recognition software, no one was untraceable.

"She's young this one."

"You're not paid to worry about that."

"This isn't a rescue mission though, right? I think

I saw something about this girl's mother a few weeks ago."

That made Viper pause. "What did you see?"

"Only that her mother had died, and Pepper's stepfather was taking over the company that should, by rights, go to this Pepper girl. We're talking a billion-dollar company. Stocks, shares, and they have stakes in pretty much everything. I'm surprised you don't know that." Maurice munched on a potato chip as he spoke.

Viper didn't follow the news. He didn't read the papers, nor did he care about pampered princesses. "Out of curiosity, what happens to this fortune if the girl dies?"

"It goes to the stepfather."

Sitting back, Viper thought about the terms of his latest contract. Pepper needed to die of natural causes, and the stepfather would inherit everything.

He didn't like the twist in his gut.

This was just another assignment like everything else, and he wasn't going to let feelings or emotions get in the way. Patting his fingers on his thigh, he watched the computer screen as faces all seemed to roll into one. This was the one part of the job that he hated.

He was bored.

When he was bored, he was able to think.

Thinking made him remember the past, and he didn't want to remember the past. He wasn't someone plagued by his fears. He had no fears.

"There she is," Maurice said.

Viper looked up as her image was brought into focus. It was a really clear image. "When was it taken?" he asked.

"Three days ago. A grocery store near the coast." Maurice rattled off several details and directions.

Viper didn't need anything else. He already knew where he was going. Pulling out a wad of cash, he handed it to Maurice, and made his way toward the door.

"Viper," Maurice said.

Turning, he saw Maurice standing, holding his keyboard. "What is it?"

"You don't have to do this, you know? She's innocent. There's nothing on her. No criminal record, nothing. Her slate is completely clean. This is not like your usual kills."

"You don't know what I've got to do, and remember, anything happens, any word gets out, and you'll die, Maurice." He wouldn't want to kill the man in front of him. Even though he was a slob, he kind of liked him, and that wasn't heard of much in his line of work. He shouldn't use the same man over and over again, but Maurice had proven himself, and he didn't want to lose a valuable asset.

"See you soon," Maurice said.

Viper was already out of the door, but he heard it.

****

Pepper stared out at the ocean, wondering if she would be able to stay here for another couple of days. It was a quaint, little town near the sea, and it was home to a lot of tourism. The beach where she stood right now was completely covered with people, with families. Would she be safe here?

She didn't know how far her father was willing to push everything. He wanted money. She knew that. From the moment her mother, her sweet, beautiful mother, had brought him home, Pepper had seen through him. He'd been a gold-digger. A horrible excuse for a human being. She had even seen him cheating on her mother with one of the staff. That had really sickened her, and what she hated most, her mother hadn't believed her.

Yes, Pepper came from a rich family, but her relationship with her mother had always been solid.

When her father died, they'd had each other, until this monster came out of nowhere, and was intent on destroying them. She hated him to her core, and that didn't help. Even when the abuse and violence had started, her mother hadn't been able to see past her own insecurity.

Then, of course, Pepper had to run, and now she couldn't even go home for her mother's funeral.

In order to gain the fortune, her stepfather needed her dead. She wasn't an idiot. All he'd wanted all along was her mother's fortune, and when Pepper died, it would all go to him.

A gust of wind hit her, and she held onto the hat, making sure it didn't blow off. She was wearing a hat and a pair of glasses. With her image over the news, she didn't want anyone to see her. Fortunately, there wasn't an updated picture, and she looked nothing like she did when she was fifteen. The picture was a cold reminder of the last time she was happy, when her mother was happy. She should probably dye her blonde hair, but it grieved her to change the locks that her mother spent hours lovingly caring for. They would sit in her father's study, and her mother would brush her hair, waiting for him to finish. Pepper looked similar to her mother, only lighter, and fairer-skinned. She burned easily in the sun, and always had to use sun lotion, which she hated wearing.

She remembered her mother rubbing the awful stuff all over her, saying if she wasn't careful she'd burn to a crisp. Then she would watch her mother do it herself. It was amazing how touching, how meaningful those memories were. At the time, they were just a nuisance, but now it was something more.

Pushing those thoughts to the back of her mind, she turned away from the sight of the ocean, and began to walk back to the main path.

The scent of doughnuts, fried chicken, and fries was heavy in the air. She wasn't hungry, and even if she was, she wouldn't eat outside.

Her stepfather was a vicious man, and would probably find some way to hurt her. She wouldn't put it past him to send someone to kill her. Were there companies like that? She didn't know. There was a lot about the world that she didn't know, and that scared her. Leaving the busy streets, she made her way back to the tiny hotel that she had rented. Without looking back, she made her way toward her door, and paused. Her door was open, and she frowned.

Hadn't she locked it?

Her heart started to pound.

It may not have locked.

Every time I left this room I locked the door.

She needed to turn around and leave.

But her stuff was in that room, and she needed to get it.

"It's fine. Everything is fine."

She gasped, and would have screamed if a hand hadn't closed over her mouth. "I suggest you be very quiet. I'm not the most patient of men, and I don't like to be kept waiting."

She couldn't see, and with how tightly he held her, she couldn't move. There was no way to get away, or for her to see who her attacker was.

He shoved her into the room, and the door slammed open, hitting the wall behind it.

Her attacker moved his hand, giving her a chance to bite him, so she did. She sank her teeth into the flesh of his hand, and made sure she didn't stop until she tasted blood.

Gross. Gross. Gross.

Disease.

She spat his hand out, stamped her foot down hard on his, and then shoved him away.

He shouted, and before she could get away, he grabbed hold of her hair, throwing her against the wall. The impact startled her, and she went a little dizzy. Within seconds he was on her. He punched her in the face, shocking her from the impact, and she rolled away. Her attacker drew back his foot, and she grabbed it, lifting it up so that he stumbled back.

Getting to her feet, she tried for the door, but he caught her again.

"You fucking fat bitch," he said, wrapping his arms around her neck, and he started to cut off her circulation.

She clawed at his arms, struggling to breathe.

"Now, isn't this interesting?" a man said.

They turned, and she saw someone who was twice the size of the man strangling her, and looked ten times as deadly.

The first thing she noticed was that he had guns at his waistband. The next thing was how calm he looked while she was getting hurt.

"Who the fuck are you?" the guy behind her asked.

"Me? I'm here on a job. Why the fuck are you here?"

"Got a job. This bitch needs to be taken out."

The man at the door laughed. "Tell me you don't have a clue who I am. Do you have any idea who I work for?"

The man behind her stilled, and the hand at her throat actually eased, surprising her. He didn't let her go, but she was able to think, and for that she was thankful.

"Viper!"

The smile on the man at the door turned deadly.

"Exactly. Now, tell me who the fuck hired you."

"Her stepfather. Who else would? He wants her gone, and he wants it done as soon as possible. Doesn't matter who gets it done so long as she's dead at the end of it."

The man called Viper looked at her as if he was assessing her. "You're really worth that much?" Viper entered the room, and closed the door. "Let the girl go, and I'll let you leave here with your life."

Laughter made her jump as the man behind her erupted as if it was the funniest thing he had ever head. "I know you've got a good reputation, Viper, but I don't think you can take me."

"Put the girl down, and let's see." Viper stood with his hands behind his back, looking so calm.

The man behind her was strong. She didn't want either man to win, but she didn't want the one behind her to win at all. That bastard was going to hurt her.

Viper was going to hurt her as well, but she hadn't actually been hurt by him yet. He was the best bet.

She was shoved down hard on the floor.

"Stay."

The man walked toward Viper, and she didn't know what she was expecting. Maybe a fight, something that was scary. She didn't expect Viper to reach out, grab the man's neck, and in one twist, snap it.

Her heart raced.

Her attacker was on the floor with his head at an odd angle. "Now this is curious." Viper began to rummage through the guy's pockets, and when he found the wallet, tossed it at her. "Who is he?"

She stared at him. "I'm not touching that."

"Tell me who he is or I'll hurt you a hell of a lot more than this bastard ever did, and from the look of your face, he hit you a few times." Viper glared at her. "Now, who is he?"

Grabbing the wallet, she opened it up, and stared at the name. "It says William Donald."

He stepped back, and grabbed his cell phone. She stared at him, and then at the door. She was in pain, hurting in places she didn't think it was possible. Could she make it out in time?

Chapter Two

This wasn't what Viper expected to find. Some asshole was moving in on his hit. Well, he *was*. Now he'd have to deal with cleaning up two dead bodies. Killer of Kings definitely had some explaining to do.

"Who the fuck is William Donald?"

Boss made an exasperated sound into the phone. "He's a free agent. Why?"

"A few minutes ago he was trying to kill my mark. I thought this was exclusive," said Viper. He glared at the girl when he saw her eyeing the door.

"You know I'd never pull that kind of underhanded shit. The stepfather must have hired him."

"He hired you. Why would he take out two contracts?" It didn't make sense. The old bastard was as greedy as they came. Maurice said he'd killed his own wife to inherit her fortune. So why pay two hitmen to knock off the stepdaughter?

"Yeah, that's one question I intend to find out. If Bernard Sutherland thinks he can hire a cheap hit to get out of paying the five million he owes me, he's got another thing coming," said Boss, his voice taking on a sinister edge. "I'll be in touch. I assume William is no longer with us?"

"You have to ask? Hurry up and get your house together. I don't want to be here longer than I need to be." He turned off his cell and shoved it in the pocket of his leather jacket. Now he had to tend to little Miss Pepper. He couldn't kill her yet, not until he got confirmation he'd be paid in full for the job. So until he got word from Boss, he'd have to lay low with the target.

"Please don't hurt me," Pepper whispered, still stomach-down on the floor, propped up on her elbows.

He ignored her.

Viper stood over the dead body, pleased with his kill. Guns and knives were fast and simple, but he hated cleaning up the blood. A broken neck was much easier to deal with. He shrugged off his jacket and hooked it over the back of a chair. Then he bent over and lugged the dead weight of the body up over his shoulder before standing. William was heavier than he looked.

He planned to store the body in the bathtub for now, but he didn't want Pepper out of his sight for a second. She was a feisty one, and he had no doubt she'd make a break for the door once he left the room. After the long trip to the seaside town, he wasn't in the mood to go chasing after her.

"Open the bathroom door for me," he said. When she froze in place, he added, "This guy isn't light."

She slowly got up to her feet, never taking her eyes off him. When she flinched, he knew she was injured, but she quickly hid her discomfort. She certainly didn't look like the pic Boss had sent him. Pepper was no little girl. She was all woman now, with curves that stole his focus—not an easy accomplishment.

He followed behind her. The hotel suite was only one small room, and it smelled mustier than it looked. He already felt claustrophobic.

Pepper wore a long blue sun dress and a thin white sweater buttoned up over it. She was much smaller than he was, but most women were. As she pushed open the bathroom door, he couldn't help but check out her ass. She was shaped like an hourglass, but she certainly wasn't one to showcase her body. The only exposed skin was on her wrists and ankles. Pepper was the essence of innocence, but it wasn't his place to care one way or the other.

It pissed him off when he started to feel—anything—because he'd been taught to remain emotionally vacant under even the harshest of conditions. As much as he despised the fuckers who'd trained him as a child, their lessons were deeply ingrained in the man he was today. He'd been called a cold-hearted bastard too many times to count, but he'd never been offered sympathy, so why should he offer it to anyone else?

He unceremoniously dropped the body into the tub with a hollow thud, and then pulled the shower curtain shut. Viper would deal with removal later. Right now, he needed to secure the hotel room and get his shit together. He hadn't planned on complications. His hits usually played out like clockwork, in and out, no time to reflect. Now he had to hole up with this girl until he got word from Killer of Kings.

After pulling the bathroom door shut tight, he pointed to the sofa. She followed directions well, taking a seat as told. "Be smart and stay put."

He locked the front door and peered out the window before tugging the heavy curtains together. A cascade of dust rained to his boots. He scanned the ceiling for any surveillance equipment, but there was nothing, not that he expected anything high tech in this shithole. Viper paced the impossibly small room, feeling like a caged tiger. He remembered the confinement exercises he was forced to endure as a young boy, and the memories both wounded him and soothed him at once. He was one twisted fuck.

"Are you going to kill me?" she asked.

He stopped half-stride, and faced her. By now, his victims usually lacked a heartbeat, so he wasn't comfortable chatting with a living one. The number one rule that had been drilled into him, one he continued to value, was never to get close to his victims. Not only did it make a killer weak, it gave them a vulnerability for others to exploit.

Viper winked. "We'll see."

She didn't look scared like he expected. Usually people lost their humanity when death was inevitable, promising him anything, or breaking into hysterics. Pepper had a calmness about her that was unusual and intriguing.

"It's my stepfather, right? He hired you."

"I don't discuss business with my targets," he said.

She kept eying his weapons. Viper was always well strapped.

"Why do you need so many guns?" she asked.

"Why not?" He pulled his Glock from his right holster and twirled in around a finger. She gasped, her body going stiff. "I'm not killing you yet, so relax." He put the handgun back in place.

Pepper shook her head. "I don't like guns, but I'm not afraid to die."

"Everyone's afraid to die. Trust me, when the time comes you'll be begging like the rest of them."

She kept quiet after that, hugging herself, and occasionally touching her face. That piece of shit must have really clocked her good. Her right cheek was already darkening, easily noticeable against her fair skin. He removed his shoulder holster and gun belt, resting them on the dinette table. Viper rolled out his shoulders and cracked his neck to each side. It had been a long day for him. He approached the skittish girl on the sofa, brushing her hair aside to assess the bruising.

"Do you like killing people?" she asked. This girl was too chatty for his liking.

"Where're you hurt?"

"I'm fine," she said, leaning away from his touch.

"He hit your face, anything else? Did he fuck you?"

Her mouth fell agape. "No," she snapped. She looked down now, a mix of shyness and embarrassment. He twirled a lock of her hair around his finger. She was cute when mad, like an angry kitten, and his teasing had the desired effect. Pepper smacked his hand.

He knelt down on one knee in front of her, snatching both her wrists in one of his fists when she attempted to swat him again. "Brave little thing. I guess you're used to getting your way, aren't you, princess?"

"What's that supposed to mean?"

He scoffed. "I hear you were raised with a silver spoon in your mouth. It'll make killing you a hell of a lot easier. So, yeah, I might enjoy this." Viper couldn't stand rich bitches. But more than anything, he was looking to get a rise out of Pepper.

"You know *nothing* about me," she said, futilely trying to tug her arms back. "I haven't done anything wrong!"

Viper stared at her, while holding her steady. *Such a waste to kill her*, he thought. Her blue eyes had flecks of gold, and her blonde hair fell over her shoulders in long, loose waves. She looked like a fucking angel, and what was he? A devil? Something about her brought down his hackles. Part of him wished this was a rescue mission and not a hit.

"What made you run?" he asked. It was a legitimate question. He wanted to know how this innocent girl could get caught up in such a mess. It was hard to imagine a delicate thing like her surviving on her own, with no one to protect her.

She didn't answer right away, her eyes welling up with unshed tears. "He started beating me, making my life miserable. If I told my mother, he said he'd kill both of us. It got so bad that I had no choice but to leave. I only found out about my mom from the news."

This time he let her have her arms back. She cupped her face with her hands and started crying, a floodgate unleashed. She was more upset remembering her mother's death than the fact he planned to kill her. He couldn't even imagine what it would feel like to be that attached to one person. Her emotional outburst made him uncomfortable, so he walked to the other side of the room to check his cell phone. Still no damn call from Boss. Pepper's sobs filled the room—holy shit, he needed some air.

He reached to put his cell back in his pocket, when it vibrated. Viper looked at the screen. It was a damn text message, and Killer of Kings strictly contacted him by phone call.

****

Pepper used the sleeve of her sweater to wipe her tears away. She didn't want this hitman to think she was weak, because he already assumed she was spoiled. Why did she even care what he thought of her? She watched him standing over the table full of weapons, his face grimacing when he checked his phone. He was huge. When he'd taken off his leather jacket, she couldn't believe the size of his muscles. He was covered in ink, intricate black patterns intertwined with skulls and demons.

Viper was the exact type of man her mother had warned her to stay away from, but for some reason she'd never felt such a powerful attraction. He had to be at least a decade older. She hated herself for desiring a man fit for nightmares, but she couldn't control her body. Pepper wasn't so sure of her mind either. She couldn't stop imagining what it would be like if a man like Viper loved her. He'd be able to protect her from the world, from her stepfather.

"Are you done with the tears?" he asked.

21

She scowled.

He peered out the curtains briefly. "*Fuck.* Pack your shit, we're leaving."

"What? Where?" Being taken to a second location was always a bad idea when it came to kidnappings—she knew that much. She didn't like the sound of being taken to a strange place, probably where he planned to murder her. Then she thought better. If he took her out in public, she'd be able to make a scene or run away. It was a very touristy area.

He started strapping all those scary weapons back on. But as much as guns terrified her, he looked so badass, so damn sexy. *What's wrong with you, Pepper?* Maybe she had daddy issues. Or she'd lost her mind completely.

"You've got two minutes, sweetheart. I suggest you get your ass moving."

Pepper hadn't taken much when she left home. She'd run off in the middle of the night with only a backpack.

"Where are we going?" she repeated. "You don't have to do this, you know. I can disappear and my stepfather won't know you didn't kill me."

He tugged his jacket on, then checked the clip on one of his guns before replacing it on his belt. "Remember that asshole in the bathroom? Well, he's not the only one." Viper strode over to her. He was so tall, she had to crane her neck to look him in the eyes. "You're welcome to stay here and take your chances with the two thugs scoping out your room, or you can come with me. I promise, I'm not as sadistic. I'm known for my swift kills."

"I don't like either of those options." She crossed her arms over her chest, but still knew she'd prefer a fast death over a painful death if those were her only choices.

But somewhere deep down inside of her, she hoped that Viper wouldn't be able to go through with killing her.

"I was trying to be nice, but this isn't a debate, princess. It's time to go."

"But—"

He growled as he turned to face her again, but he still appeared collected. Her stepfather had always been in a perpetual rage, and he terrified her. Not Viper. "What is it now?"

"I'm scared," she admitted. Pepper didn't want to appear weak, but the thought of two hitmen outside waiting to kill her was a terrifying prospect. This was crazy, too much for her to process. Pepper wanted to withdraw within herself, to hide from all the evil in the world. "What if one of them shoots me?"

He exhaled and ran a hand through his dark hair. "Is that all? As long as you're with me, I guarantee you'll be safe from them."

She could hear something right outside the door, and she saw the knob move. Adrenaline scattered like wildfire through her veins. She pointed, unable to speak.

"Relax. You've been on the run for months, so I know you're stronger than this. Just keep quiet. Got it?"

Pepper nodded. She had the overwhelming urge to throw herself into his arms. Now that her mother was dead, she didn't have a soul to turn to for comfort. She'd never felt so scared and alone.

"Hey." His leather jacket creaked as he tilted her chin up. The scent of his woodsy cologne was pure masculinity. "Be a good girl for me, okay?" She studied him. He had a unique intensity, and a gnarly scar that cut down the length of his face on one side. She imagined most women would be repelled, but his imperfections were somehow beautiful to her. Pepper wondered if he ever smiled.

He put his finger to his lips to silence her as he backed away from her toward the door. Viper stood behind it, and ever so carefully unlocked the deadbolt. She couldn't believe he was going to invite the murderers in without a fight. To make matters worse, her feet turned to lead. She froze in place when she needed to take cover.

Someone kicked in the door a moment later, two men rushing into the room with guns raised. The first man had grey hair and a pot belly. He smiled when he saw her standing there, like a deer in the headlights. She still couldn't move.

"So good to see you, Pepper." He had a raspy smoker's voice. As he approached her, he tucked his gun away and began to slip on a pair of gloves. She watched as he wiggled each chubby finger in, one at a time.

The other guy was muscle-bound, his black suit too tight. He spilled the contents of a plastic bag on the table. There were syringes and baggies of white powder.

"Take off your sweater," said the older man. "Let me see your arms."

Her heart felt like it was being squeezed in a vise. She couldn't even breathe. When she looked to Viper, still standing in the dark shadow behind the door, he put his finger to his lips again. She swallowed her paralyzing fear, unbuttoned her sweater, and slipped it off. Pepper always wore sweaters, even in the heat, because she didn't want to showcase her extra weight and thick arms. Growing up, the women in their elite circle were picture-perfect and highly critical of anything less than perfection. She never felt like she belonged.

The man grabbed her wrist in a bruising grip, pulling her arm straight. "Shit, she's not a user."

The big guy came over, flicking a full syringe with a finger. "Too late to worry about that now. Besides, there's always a first time for everyone—especially grieving daughters."

Pepper began to hyper-ventilate, rearing back, trying to get her arm free.

"Don't you know drugs are bad for your health?"

The older guy turned his head to the voice, and Viper delivered a short straight-punch to his face, followed by an elbow, and another punch. Each move was precise and effective, knocking the man to the ground. Viper's hulking presence was all-business, his eyes black and flat.

When the big guy with the needle charged him, Pepper screamed, "Viper!"

But he didn't need her help. He twisted the other man in a headlock so fast, it was almost inhuman. He hit him in such a brutal fashion, she had to look away. Blood sprayed the carpet, and a gross gurgling sound was followed by the heavy body falling to the ground.

The older man on the floor attempted to get back up. Pepper didn't even think, kicking him sharply in the ribs. Unfortunately, she wasn't as proficient as her hitman. He grabbed her leg, and she toppled down beside him. Pepper flailed her arms as he tried to strike her.

The sound of a gun cocking ended the struggle. Viper stood over the other man. He pressed the muzzle firm to his forehead. "Name. Now."

"Giovanni Bianchi."

"Who hired you?"

There was a pause. "He didn't tell me his name."

Viper pistol-whipped him, hard, then returned the gun to his head. "Last chance. Tell me something."

The old man began sobbing. "It was supposed to look like an overdose. That's all I know, I swear."

Viper shifted his attention to her, not moving his position. "Turn your head."

She did as he told her, and then the blast of a

gunshot shocked her to the core. Pepper curled up in a ball and screamed.

Moments later, strong hands pried her fingers from face. "Open your eyes, Pepper."

She peeked up to find Viper standing over her. He returned his gun to his holster, then reached down to hoist her effortlessly up to her feet. "Are they dead?" she asked.

He nodded, his hands still on her sides under her arms. They were so close. The room was quiet enough to hear the wall clock ticking, every second matching the rapid beat of her heart. "You tried to help me," he said, barely above a whisper.

Pepper shrugged. "I didn't want him to hurt you."

No one had ever looked at her the way Viper did just now. He saw beyond the surface, maybe all the way to her soul, a look of disbelief making the corners of his eyes crinkle.

"You're a complication," he said, no hint of emotion. God, she hoped for more from him. She was a mess, a basket-case of emotional instability. Pepper needed to be reassured, comforted, anything. How could he be so numb? Was he a complete sociopath?

The brief moment of silence and what she optimistically perceived as intimacy was doused when Viper's cellphone rang. He pulled away so abruptly she felt dizzy.

"About time," he answered.

After listening for a minute, he froze, turning to look at her as he lowered the hand holding the cell. For the first time, she swore she saw a brief wave of emotion behind in his dark eyes. She knew what it was because it kept her sleepless most nights—regret.

Chapter Three

"Don't you ever send me a fucking text again!" Viper made sure he got that out before he forgot. There were only a few words that he'd been able to make out, and that was because they were the only words he'd known: more, kill, money. Three words, and everything else had meant nothing to him.

Yeah, it was fucking hilarious.

No one knew his weakness, not even Boss. When he had joined the corporation, he had demanded that all correspondence be done via phone call. No one had argued with him. Gritting his teeth, he looked back into the hotel room. It seemed that darling step-daddy hired as many people as possible to make sure that she disappeared permanently.

This was going to be a harder mess to clean up.

"Did you phone me to bitch, or do you need something?" Boss asked. "I take it the complications are dead?"

"Of course they are. The room is registered in her name. Our bright little princess didn't think to use an alias. That's what created this complication."

Boss swore.

"Any chance he's paid up what money he owes you?" he asked.

"Nope. Bastard is conveniently not returning my calls. She stays alive until I give you further notice. I want your exact location, and I'll send in the cleaning crew. You will need to wrap them up, and I'll handle disposal."

"Got it." He hung up the cell phone, and stared at the mess. "Your stepfather wants you dead. What he doesn't seem to have figured out is that the moment you put a mass fucking hit on one person, the likelihood of them making it look natural is out the fucking window."

"So you're going to kill me?" she asked.

He didn't like how his gut twisted at her words. "Yes." There was no point in lying to the girl, and that was what he had to remember, she was a girl. No, she was a fucking target. He needed to remember that more importantly. "Luckily for you, your stepfather is a total asshole, and so that means you get to live a little longer, Miss Pepper."

"Don't call me that. My mom called me that. Don't do that."

Viper watched as tears fell from her eyes but this time they were not accompanied by sobbing. He found this entire situation a massive clusterfuck. This was why he rarely took jobs with multiple contracts. Viper didn't care what the other men at Killer of Kings did. This was strictly his deal. It got messy quickly, and then the fighting among fellow mercenaries just made it uglier. Moving toward his backpack, he pulled out the emergency bath towel, and placed it on the floor. He always had his survival 101 kit. A shower curtain might not be the obvious choice, but for him it had worked far too many times to leave it out. He spread it on the floor, and then took each man, one by one, and dumped their asses. Grabbing a set of cuffs from his pocket, he walked over to Pepper. She shrank away from him.

He didn't like that, but rather than dwell on that feeling, he grabbed her wrist, and secured it to the bed far away from the door.

"You're just going to chain me up?"

"Some women would find that kinky." She gritted her teeth, and looked away from him. "You thinking all kinds of kinky shit now?" he asked.

"Fuck you."

"You never know. Your stepfather doesn't come

through I may do exactly that, and keep you alive." He stroked a finger down her cheek, and she pulled away. However, he saw the response of her body. Those big tits and large nipples showed her arousal. It certainly wasn't cold in the room, and he had sweat coming off him. Now that was interesting. He wouldn't delve into that just yet. Right now, she wasn't his target, but she also wasn't his enemy. "Until I know what I'm doing, your life is in my hands either way. Behave, and do as you're told." The strangest urge to kiss her came over him, and he shoved it away.

Kissing her wouldn't resolve anything, and it would only confuse an already shitty situation. It was something he never did because it raised the stakes too high.

After securing the cuff around her wrist, he moved away, and stared at the men he'd killed. They had been good. Drugging her and making it look like an overdose was smart. Girl had just lost her mother and all that, but he didn't like it. He didn't like how they had been able to get so close.

He wouldn't have let them plunge that nasty shit into her veins. Being the recipient of forced drugs himself, he knew how bad it could get, and he wasn't into it. Not at all.

"More people are on the way?" she asked.

"Yes. It would seem you're a valuable asset. I'm surprised you're not trying to, you know, barter for your life."

"How could I barter? I don't have anything to give." She snorted. "Unless you call my virginity a bartering tool, I'm all out."

"So you're a virgin then?" he asked, glancing over at her.

Her cheeks were a lovely shade of red, and she

rolled her eyes. "I've got nothing to offer you."

"I don't know. I've never fucked a virgin before."

"Yeah, and that's worth the millions of dollars you're being paid to hunt me down, and kill me?" she asked.

"You're right, it's not worth the same. To some guy it would be." He wasn't that guy. Chancing another look at her, he saw her head was bowed and she was staring at her dress, which had ridden up. Getting to his feet, he held the edge of her dress, and pulled it back over her thighs and knees, giving her the comfort she wanted.

Without saying a word, he entered the bathroom and grabbed the other dead body. Heaving him over his shoulder, he walked back into the bedroom, and dropped him onto the pile of dead bodies.

Then he moved toward the curtain, and pulled it back enough for him to look out. He'd gone from killing to babysitting. Boss wouldn't be long now, and then he'd get to make his decision.

"Do you know if my mom suffered?" Pepper asked.

"I don't know anything about her death. I don't watch the news, I don't read reports. I was told that I had a hit on you, and that's why I'm here."

She sniffled, and he tensed.

Viper expected her to start talking about her dead mom, and he waited for it, but nothing came out.

Pulling out his Glock, he checked outside again, waiting for Boss's crew to come. Once the bodies were disposed of, he'd take the girl, and wait for further instructions. This was a rather unique situation. He'd never been with a woman this long unless he was going to fuck her.

He closed the curtain, and he noticed she was still looking down at her lap as if it was the most fascinating thing in the world.

"You loved your mom?" he asked, and then started to curse himself. This wasn't part of his job description. He killed. He didn't ask questions.

"Yes, I did. I know you think it's stupid, but I do. I mean, I did." She shook her head. "Ignore me."

"Your stepfather wants you dead. You know why?"

"He only wants my family's money and inheritance. Both my parents were wealthy, and their company became unstoppable. My dad died in a boating accident about five years ago." She shrugged. "Then that monster arrived, and everything changed. My mom just wanted someone to love and to have someone to love her. It doesn't matter. You probably think it's stupid."

He did. That was the worst thing about the entire situation. He didn't give a shit about why she was here, but he couldn't help but feel sorry for her. "I'm sorry for your loss."

"Thank you."

Silence fell between them. He liked silence. When there was stillness it allowed him to control everything, and when he was the one in charge, nothing bad happened. In his mind, he started to count. It was the only thing he had. Counting was something he was allowed to do, what he'd been trained to do. Without the ability to do math, he couldn't guarantee that he'd been paid right.

Why the fuck are you thinking about this shit?

Target.

Kill.

Money.

Move on.

It was the life he'd been leading for a long time now, and one he wasn't willing to give up on. Not even for a curvy blonde with shocking blue eyes filled with so much pain. If he focused too much on that pain, he had a desire to find the bastard responsible and kill him. He was an expert in torture, and could come up with many ways of keeping someone alive while he tormented them.

****

Pepper wiped her tears away. The pain in her head was excruciating. Until her stepfather had arrived, life seemed to have moved on, to be the same. It had always been her, her mother, and father. Then when he died, it had just been her and her mom.

The beatings, the cruelty, that hadn't started until her mother had become weak. One day her mother had this ethereal beauty. She was a sweet, charismatic, and beautiful soul. The next day she seemed unable to form simple sentences, becoming weak, frail, and a complete shell of her former self. Little by little, Pepper had watched her become lifeless. With her mother bedbound, it had given that monster a chance to hurt Pepper in every possible way but one. He'd never raped her, and for that she was thankful. From the way he looked at her though, she knew he didn't like her *that* way. She was too big, too much of a woman for him as far as she was concerned. With her mother gone, she wasn't going to let anyone else rule or control her.

She had to fight back.

Barter with Viper.

Everyone had probably been able to do this, and yeah, she was going to be another one.

"How much did my stepfather pay you?"

"Does that really matter?" Viper asked. His back was to her and he held a gun in his hand, ready to do business whenever he needed to. She had watched him snap a guy's neck. He really didn't need the gun.

"Well, I'm just thinking. He needs me dead to inherit my family's fortune, right? So I'm like, in charge of it. I know it's a lot because I'm one of the wealthiest heiresses out there. It said so on the television."

"What are you getting at?"

She licked her lips, and took a deep breath. "I want to pay you twice as much as him to keep me alive."

Viper threw back his head and laughed. "Yeah, right. As soon as I get the call from Boss, you're dead."

"Really? Do you think a man with absolutely no money to his name can pay your fee?" she asked. "Think about it, Viper. You're clever, right? He's nobody. He married and killed by mother. No second spouse can inherit. That fortune is mine. Everything belongs to me, unless I die. He's living in my family's house with a few grand they keep out of the safe. Even if she gave him the bank details to her money, he couldn't access it. It changes, and I have all the necessary codes to get it."

When her father had explained how they kept the fortune safe, she hadn't believed it. Everything seemed a little farfetched, but then again, it was a modern-day world. She had the codes and the means of getting money. It was why she could go on the run. She knew all she had to do was go into any bank, to get what she needed. "Why don't you call your friend back? See if the funds have cleared, and if I'm lying."

She rested her head against the wall as he did exactly that.

You cannot be attracted to him.
He's a monster just like the man you ran from.
Fight this.
Get some balls, and fight him.
Win.

"Hey, Boss. Yeah, I got everything covered and all, but I was just wondering if any of that money had cleared?"

She didn't hear the response, but she saw his grip

tighten on the gun.

"Well, little miss pampered has a proposal." Viper moved toward her, and handed out the phone. "Talk to him."

"Hello," she said.

"Pepper, I'm curious. How did you know the money wouldn't clear?"

"He has no means of sending it. He's broke, whoever you are. I'm the only one with access. My father, my grandfather, and older generations implemented this. They made sure no gold-digger could have what didn't belong to them."

"You've intrigued me. What do you want?"

"I want to stay alive. I know he wants me dead, but I've done nothing wrong."

"I'm not in the market of keeping people alive." His words hung in the air, and what little hope she had started to disappear. "But I've been known to change when I need to. Just because it's not a specialty doesn't mean I can't improvise. Put Viper on the phone."

She handed the phone back to Viper.

Watching him talk, she wondered if she had bought herself some time. She wasn't lying. She had access to that money, and could use it whenever she needed it. But she couldn't use it if she was dead.

I know you told me not to do anything stupid when I finally inherited, Dad. I think surviving is a good reason to spend a lot of it.

Viper closed his phone. "You have yourself a deal. Boss will text you the details. The moment he does, you transfer funds, and it will be activated, and I will do everything in my power to protect you."

Her cell phone beeped. "I need my phone."

The thing about her stepfather was he seemed to be too good at acting, and it made everyone believe him.

How could a nice guy be so mean? She had felt his evil and knew now to always be on guard.

After getting the information she needed, Pepper did the necessary transactions, and sent the money that would guarantee her safety. It was time for her to fight the asshole who had been hurting her for longer than he should have.

Why should she just roll over and play dead for a man who didn't deserve a dime of her inheritance?

Viper's phone rang.

He was close enough that she could hear the other man.

"She's right. The fucking target is right. He couldn't pay, and was hoping someone would carry out the hit, and then he could pay. Fucker is playing a dangerous game here, Viper. He's not smart."

"Her funds clear?" Viper asked.

"Of course they have. Save the girl at all costs. She's just paid us ten million, and according to the little side note she gave me, you succeed in saving her, there's another ten. Keep her alive."

The call ended, and Viper closed his phone. He stared at her from across the room. "You've surprised me. Not so long ago you were willing to die."

"I changed my mind." She'd thought about her mother, and then her father. He wouldn't have wanted her to give up, and especially not to a man who had killed to get where he was.

"You've surprised me, and that's a compliment. I don't get surprised very easily." He took a seat on the edge of the bed, not taking his eyes off her.

Licking her dry lips, she averted her gaze. "I don't suppose you'd let me go now?"

"I thought you wanted protection?" he asked. "Suit yourself. You wouldn't last five minutes out there.

It would seem your stepdad knows how to make people do what he wants."

"I didn't mean for me to go. I'm not leaving your side." Why did that suddenly sound very sexual? She took a deep breath, and smiled. "I meant from being chained to this bed. I'm not going anywhere. I've paid you guys a lot of money to keep me alive, and I won't back out. I do want to live."

She didn't like how her body came alive under Viper's perusal. Her nipples tightened, and her pussy grew slick, and it was entirely inappropriate. There were dead men lying a few feet away. Men that had wanted to kill her, to drug her up and make her death look like a suicide. Totally not an original idea.

She tensed as he stood and advanced toward her. For him it was just a few short strides. If it was her, it would have been a few more. He was just so much bigger than she was. Clenching her teeth, she tried not to show her body's reaction to his closeness.

It's totally fine.

He's just a handsome, sexy, stranger.

Who happens to be protecting you from your very insane stepfather.

The moment his hand touched hers, her entire body felt alive like it was being awakened for the first time. Opening her eyes, which had magically closed, she found him only a breath away, staring right at her.

Did his gaze go to her lips? Did he want to kiss her?

Crap. She hadn't brushed her teeth. Her face hurt as well. What if he kissed her, and she hated it because of the pain?

Shut up, and just take the kiss.

The kiss didn't happen. He stepped away and returned to the window. Glancing down, she saw he had removed the cuffs, and placed them in her lap. He'd been so gentle as he touched her, she hadn't even realized he'd freed her.

Men had never been nice to her. She pushed all the bad memories away. Pepper didn't need to remind herself of the hell she'd endured the past few months.

"I believe your mother went peacefully," he said.

"I'm sorry? You said you didn't know."

"I have ways of getting information. She went peacefully in her sleep so you don't have to worry about that."

"Thank you," she said. Deep down she knew he didn't have the real answers. "Is this new for you?"

"What?"

"Saving your targets? You know, the change of mission or whatever it is you call it?" she asked.

"You're the first kill that I now have to protect. Look, don't expect much small talk out of me. It's not going to happen."

When he glanced in her direction, the moonlight casting a glow into the bedroom, she saw his scars just before he turned his head.

"How did you get your scars?"

He didn't move a muscle or say anything. His gaze wasn't even on her but on the street now. Nothing about his posture gave away his thoughts, or even if he'd heard the question.

"Boss's crew is here," he said.

Within minutes there was a bang on the door, and then there wasn't time for her to say anything else.

Chapter Four

The cleaning crew was his saving grace. He wasn't good with emotionally tense situations, and the longer he talked with Pepper, the more she managed to weaken him. It would be easy if he didn't give a shit about her, but for some reason he did. Was it her innocence? The fact she didn't belong in his black and white world? Or maybe it was the way she turned him on without even trying? Whatever the fuck it was, he needed to man up and get over it before she destroyed him.

"How's it hanging, Viper?" Spade strolled into the room, a black garbage back slung casually over his shoulder. Lola followed behind him with a mop and bucket.

"Things could be better," Viper said. "Anyway, there're just the three of them there. One gunshot."

There were numerous crews that handled clean-up, depending on the location. He was usually cleaner, no blood, but when he'd seen that asshole put his hands on Pepper, he'd lost it.

"Who's the chick?" asked Lola.

"Don't worry about her," he said. Pepper was watching from her spot on the bed, not saying a word. She looked like a fish out of water. He imagined Miss Fancy Pants was used to tea parties and book clubs. Now she was fighting for her life in the shittiest hotel room he'd seen in a long time.

"We'll have this finished fast if you want to take off," said Spade.

"Boss not coming around?"

Spade shook his head. "He texted me the address, that's it."

Viper sure as hell wasn't going to stick around in the same hotel. He'd already killed three men and had no doubt more would come out of the woodwork. When money was involved, all the free agents competed for the bounty. It was late now, the time when darkness cast a concealing shadow on the criminal underworld. It would be a feeding frenzy with Pepper's death as the prize. Viper's job wasn't as simple—he had to protect her from all those boogeymen.

"This is the girl from the news, isn't it?" Lola asked. Viper hadn't noticed her walk over the bed. She flicked Pepper's hair with disregard. "I don't see what all the fuss is about."

He didn't want to appear attached to his mark, so he ignored Lola's behavior.

Spade was busy securing the bodies. He was a big, burly, no-nonsense kind of man. Viper could appreciate someone who did their job with professionalism and little chatter.

Lola unzipped her jacket and tossed it on the sofa. She wore a tight black cat suit underneath. "I was hoping it was *your* clean-up when Boss called," she said, approaching him. "It's been way too long, Viper." Lola dragged a finger down the center of his chest.

He didn't move. And he wasn't impressed. Viper wasn't the kind of man to fall for the wiles of a woman. Lola was deeply rooted in their lifestyle, with a reputation to match, and he didn't plan on mixing business with pleasure. Besides, she wasn't his type.

"Do you have to babysit her all night, or can you get away for a while?" she asked, looking up at him with anticipation. Viper wasn't a saint. If he was in the mood, he'd fuck any willing woman. But why should he settle for a skinny bitch with fake tits when he had a real woman only a few feet away? Of course, the fact Pepper was a virgin and hated his guts wasn't going to help him get lucky any time soon.

"We were just leaving," Viper said. "Spade, this address is hot, so watch your back."

"Always."

He used a curled finger to signal Pepper to come. She made a wide arch around the bodies and walked toward him, a slight limp in her step.

"Ready to go?" he asked her.

She nodded. He could practically feel her discomfort as she sidled up next to him. She was so fucking cute.

Lola crossed her arms, glaring at Pepper with a look of pure evil. "I know Viper. Trust me, he doesn't want you. You're just a paycheck."

"Did I ask you to speak for me?" he asked.

"Am I wrong?"

"Watch yourself." Viper was tiring of this game "Don't you have a job to do?" He needed to get out of this one-horse town before more mercenaries showed up.

"I can save you the headache," Lola said. "Want me to add her to the body count? No extra charge, for you." She yanked the edge of Pepper's dress, making her gasp. It surprised him when she clung to him for security, her little fists bunching up his t-shirt. A satisfying rush took him off guard. He liked the fact Pepper sought him for protection. And not just because he was being paid to do it.

"You're starting to piss me off, Lola. Not bright." He pressed a hand to the small of Pepper's back, leading her to the entrance. "Stay close to me, okay?"

They left the hotel room. The driver for the cleaning crew kept the car idling nearby, the low beams cutting across the aged concrete. Being outside in the open air put Viper on edge. He scanned the rooftops, the streets, and assumed every passerby was a suspect. The streetlamp in front of the hotel flickered on and off in the darkness, insects clamoring to the meager light. He walked fast, looking for a suitable vehicle so they could get on the road. Pepper tried to keep up, but it was clear she had an injury or two. There was no time to stop and check on her until they were in a safe place.

"Who were those people?" she asked.

"Cleaning crew."

"That woman didn't like me very much."

Viper chuckled. "She was just jealous." He ducked to look in the passenger window of Ford Mustang. *Perfect.*

"Why would she be jealous of me? She's so perfect."

He jimmied the lock, opened the door, and dropped across the seats to get it hotwired. When the engine purred to life, he shifted into the driver's seat. "Come on, get in."

Pepper sat in the passenger seat and closed the door. Only the soft glow from the dashboard cut the darkness. "You didn't answer me," she said. "Why would she be jealous?"

He knew Pepper wasn't street smart, but for a spoiled, rich girl, she wasn't very bright. Viper turned slightly to the side. "Lola likes being the center of attention. She was pissed that I was more attracted to you than her."

"Why would she think that?"

He narrowed his eyes. Was she for real? "Because it's true."

Her lips parted as realization set in. For once she was at a loss for words. Viper hit the gas and steered his gorgeous new ride onto the roadway.

As they put distance between them and the small tourist town, the streets became barren. A light drizzle and thick cloud cover blocked out the moon and stars.

The open road, the darkness, the quiet—they were his only faithful companions over the years. Sometimes he allowed himself to wonder, to imagine how his life would differ if he'd had a normal childhood. At thirty-four, he'd probably be married with a few kids. He'd work as an accountant or maybe something with his hands. It was hard to put himself in those shoes, almost impossible to visualize himself giving and receiving love. The whole idea of family suffocated him. Why would he trade his freedom, endless traveling, and unique skillset for one woman? As much as he hated his past, maybe it was all meant to be in the grand scheme of things. There was no way he could cut it as a family man, living in the suburbs, and smiling to his asshole neighbors when they put out the garbage. No fucking way.

His thoughts betrayed him. Viper turned on the radio, the deep bass of the music creating an atmosphere of intimacy, so he shut it off just as fast. What was happening to him? If he could go back a couple days in time he'd tell Boss to take his fucking assignment and shove it up his ass. What was supposed to be a side job, a clean hit, was now turning his life upside down.

Viper thought about getting another hotel, paying cash, and laying low. But his mood was becoming uniquely vulnerable, so he needed familiar territory to get himself grounded. The shadowed landscape never seemed to change during the long drive, like a vinyl record repeating over and over.

In his peripheral vision, he noticed Pepper hugging her arms, rhythmically rubbing up and down. It was the first time she'd moved a muscle in almost an hour. Pepper had been staring blankly into nothingness, and he'd wondered if she was in shock.

"You cold?"

"I forgot my sweater."

It was one of the hottest summers on record, so he didn't see the big deal. "You can always buy another one. Remember, 'you're the wealthiest heiress out there'."

"Can you please stop?" she snapped. "I know you think I'm this rich bitch not worth saving, but you don't know me at all. Money doesn't equal happiness. I would have traded everything just to be accepted."

"I thought your mother loved you."

"Of course she did. That didn't change the fact I was the black sheep with everyone else. It's not fun being the fat kid nobody wanted in pictures. I wasn't immune to the whispers, either. You wouldn't know how that felt."

"Why would you assume that?"

She faced him, her blonde hair falling to one side. "Look at you."

He shrugged. "You think I had an easy ride?"

"Whatever."

Viper barely stifled a growl. This girl was impossible. "I can call the crew and tell them to save the fucking sweater. Would that make you happy?"

The city came into view in the distance. An endless sea of lights in the inky blackness of the countryside. He wasn't one to put down roots, but most of his time off for the past three years had been spent in the same downtown condo. It was his safe haven and as close to a home as a man like him could hope to get.

"I don't care about the dumb sweater!" she shouted, taking him off guard. He swerved out of his lane for a moment. "If you haven't noticed, I'm not exactly a prize catch, so I feel more comfortable when I'm covered up."

Viper sharply hit the brakes, pulling over to the soft shoulder of the road. The tires rumbled along the gravel until they jerked to a full stop. The earlier mist had developed into a light, steady rain. The lack of streetlamps left them in complete darkness, only the glow from the city acting as a distant night light.

"What the fuck is your problem?" he asked. "You're worried about showing me a little skin? You think I'm going to judge you?"

"Leave me alone," she said, her temper fading to nothing. Pepper undid her seatbelt and twisted away from him.

"Oh no you don't." He tugged her shoulder, forcing her to turn around. "Listen, little lady, I don't think you're fat. I don't think you need to hide your body, and the assholes who put that idea in your head can go fuck themselves." What was he doing? As much as he knew it was a mistake to engage in this conversation, he couldn't stop himself.

"It's true."

He cupped her cheek, and she twitched from the contact. It only reminded him he needed to catalogue all her injuries once they got to his place.

Their heavy breathing and the soft hum of the engine were the only sounds inside the parked car. Her skin was velvety soft, and he was careful not to add too much pressure with his hand. Nothing about Viper was soft. Everything in his life was debased, but Pepper was a little blonde ray of sunshine in his otherwise dismal world.

"I've already told you why Lola was jealous, right?"

"She just hated me. I'm used to it."

"Damn, you're stubborn." He'd have to spell it out before she believed he could possibly be attracted to her. Pepper was like his own personal kryptonite, and it took all his willpower to behave and keep his mind on the job. "Look, you don't need to cover up." He ran the backs of his fingers down the length of her bare arm. "I think you're perfect. Too perfect for me, that's for damn sure." He pulled away, taking a cleansing breath. Once this job was over, Pepper would have her whole life ahead of her. Viper would only drag her down, fill her life with darkness. The most decent thing he could do would be to keep his distance—but then again, he'd always been a bastard.

"Stop mocking me." Pepper shoved him, then opened the car door, spilling to the muddy ground. He watched in shock as she began running into the night. *Fuck!*

Viper didn't sign up for this. He gave chase, easily catching up with her. He lunged forward, wrapping an arm around her waist to bring her to a halt. She struggled, but he ignored her protests, carrying her thrashing body back to the car. "I guess we need the handcuffs again," he said.

He set her to her feet and pinned her against the side of the car with his body. Rivulets of rain tracked down his face as he stared at her. She squirmed and complained. He wanted to kill. All he'd ever known was killing. It would be so easy to strangle her into silence. Beautiful silence. But this fucking little blonde with the fragile self-esteem was his weakness. He didn't want her dead. Every cell in his body demanded he resist his killing instinct and protect her—from the world, from himself.

****

Pepper was a hot mess. She was overly tired, stressed, scared, and her self-esteem was at an all-time low. Not to mention her unacceptable attraction for Viper was growing stronger. When Lola had touched Viper at the hotel, something burned inside of Pepper. It was jealousy, white, hot, and potent. It didn't help that Lola had a figure fit for magazine covers, and Pepper was plain and pudgy. God, she wanted Viper to want her. As stupid as it sounded, it was all-consuming. When he started telling her how perfect she was, it stung. If anyone was perfect, it was the muscled Adonis staring down at her like she was a problem to solve. Pepper was anything but perfect, so he was either being an asshole or wanted to steal her virginity.

"For God's sake, Pepper…"

"Get off of me!"

"How the hell am I mocking you? By telling you you're perfect?"

"Yes, because we both know it's a lie."

She could barely struggle, his rock-hard body sandwiching her with the car. He secured both her wrists in his iron fists at the sides of her head. Her breasts were thrust up, creating mountainous cleavage at the top of her dress. He waited for her to lose steam. Part of her expected him to hit her like her stepfather had. How could a killer be so composed?

"Listen, I'm wet, I'm muddy, and it's taking all my self-control not to fuck you right here, right now. I'm trying to be a gentleman, but you have no idea the things I'd like to do to you, starting with these gorgeous tits of yours." His cock pressed against her stomach, a testament to his words.

Pepper froze, his dirty words replaying over in her head. He was so unapologetic and no holds barred. And those black, evil eyes watched her like she was something to eat, and she liked it.

This time he released her hands and leaned low to whisper in her ear. "I've been with a lot of women. They meant nothing to me." He took a deep breath at the base of her neck. "You. You drive me crazy. And I hate being out of control."

"Viper…"

He licked the trails of rain water off her cheek, and she trembled, resting her hands on his biceps. Even through his leather coat, she could feel the hardness of his muscles. "If you think I was attracted to Lola, you're wrong. I'm a big man—I need curves, and you have more than enough to keep me satisfied."

She gasped.

Viper ran his hand into her slick hair, then secured a handful, tucking her head to the side. He ran his tongue over his teeth, a feral need in his eyes. "I've never kissed a woman."

"How's that possible?"

"It's too intimate. I only fuck."

Would she be different? Could he change for her? Even a mercenary had to crave love. Didn't everyone? Pepper knew there was evil in the world, but she saw goodness in Viper. He might not admit it, but she saw something inside him worth saving.

"Maybe you should change that." She wanted him to kiss her, her entire body braced in anticipation. His lips were thick, his rough scar making him appear dangerous and unbelievably sexy. His reluctance only made her crave him more.

He released his hold on her hair, tracing the pad of his thumb along the moisture of her bottom lip. "You don't know what you're asking." When he pulled back, his fingers accidentally grazed the side of her breast. It felt like butterflies fluttering in her stomach, her flicker of arousal now blazing out of control. "I was hired to protect you. Let me do my job."

Viper held out his arm, motioning her to sit in the passenger seat. When she sat down, her pussy was achy. What was his deal? Pepper was so wound tight, she probably would have gone along with anything Viper suggested. Now she felt like an idiot. A horny idiot.

When the driver's side door slammed shut, he pumped the gas, destroying the quiet. "We'll be at our location in twenty minutes," he said, matter-of-factly.

"And where's that?"

"My condo. You can get some sleep and clean up." He steered back onto the deserted roadway, briefly fishtailing on the slick surface, not taking his eyes off the windshield. The thought of being in Viper's private domain, in his bed, didn't help her uncomfortable predicament. All she could smell was fresh rain mixed with leather and musky cologne. Pepper realized her thoughts were no longer focused on staying alive. She'd been worrying about something much more dangerous—falling for a hitman.

Chapter Five

Never in all the years he'd been a mercenary working for Killer of Kings had he invited anyone, man or woman, to his home. Viper parked in the secure underground facility. This condo was locked up tight, secure gates, parking, bullet-proof glass, and so many locks it was tighter than Fort Knox. He made sure that whenever he wasn't working, he had a place that meant he could be safe, and this was what he owned.

Taking Pepper's hand, he made his way toward the elevator, and scanned through his security. There was his thumbprint, a ten-digit code, and even a drop of his blood. Yes, he was paranoid, but he also knew how damn determined some of the other mercenaries were when a hit was ordered. At any time, he could have contracted for his own back, and this was his protection. Of course, he also made sure that he didn't piss anyone else off, but when it came to money, most people were greedy.

All he had to do was remember how they flocked to this kill. Just thinking about the men and women that were after Pepper had him tightening his hand around hers. She winced.

"You're hurting me."

And he quickly let her go. His strength was his biggest enemy.

Training for years, he had only learned to get stronger, and right beside him was a precious little princess, and he didn't even mean that derogatorily either. She was a sweet girl, and he saw kindness deep in her eyes. Back at the hotel room when Lola was scaring her, she'd reached out toward him. She didn't even have a clue that between him and Lola, he was the bigger monster.

"Sorry," he said, sucking his thumb into his

mouth, to get rid of his blood. They stood in the elevator, and he saw how pale she was. "You'll be safe here."

"You have so much security, even more than my family had. It's kind of … reassuring."

"But it scares you?"

"Doesn't it you?"

He placed a hand on her back, wishing there wasn't any fabric between them. The sudden desire to see her naked, to have her bent over the nearest counter or up against the wall was strong. Gritting his teeth, he controlled his desire, and fortunately the elevator opened. "In my line of work, you realize the risk you take, and you take precautions. If every mercenary was smart, they would have a home exactly like mine."

"It's a dangerous world that you live in."

"Kill or be killed. I'd rather be the one that's doing the killing."

"You don't feel remorse?"

"Most of the people I killed are bad people." He kept on walking but she stopped, and he turned to her.

"I'm not a bad person. I've never done anything mean to anyone in my whole life."

He saw the tears shining in her eyes, and knew this had to be shock. She was a normal woman, a rich-normal woman. She had never lived the life he had.

"It's a greedy man who wants to kill me. How many kinds of people like me have you killed? You know, for the right price?"

For the first time in his life, Viper didn't like being judged. She wasn't judging him, no. All Pepper was doing was asking a simple question.

"I don't talk about what I did, or how I did it. Come on, you're hurting, and I want to see the damage." He took her hand, and led her toward the bathroom. With her limping, he slowed down so that he didn't upset her.

All of his life he'd known pain. That was what he'd been trained to do—to hunt, to kill, and to never ask any questions.

"Do you own any books?" Pepper asked. "I don't see any."

"No."

"Oh, I love books."

Of course she did.

"Let me guess, romance."

"There's nothing wrong with loving a little romance," she said. "It makes me happy."

"Romance is just a bunch of lies."

"How would you know? I bet you've never even read one."

"I've never read any book," he said, entering his large bathroom. He loved luxury, space, and everywhere he went inside his home, there was some kind of weapon within easy reach.

He lifted her up onto his counter, and she gave a little squeal. After turning on the light, he got a good look at her bruise.

"I'm fine."

"You're not fine. You're hurting." He took hold of her chin and turned it this way and that, muttering under his breath. "That first guy really did a number on you."

She touched her face, and winced. "It does hurt."

"Yeah, there's not a lot we can do with your face." Sliding his fingers down her arm, he stared at where the men had gotten close to injecting her. There wasn't a single mark on her skin, and for that he was thankful. Just the thought of those animals putting that junk into her veins made him angry. He should have been allowed the time to torture them properly. "They didn't get to you."

"It was close."

"I know. I wouldn't have let them actually put that shit in your veins."

"How were you going to kill me then?" she asked. "Huh?"

"You know? I need to die of natural causes. The drug overdose seems natural. A daughter's guilt over losing her mother, and not being there. How would you have killed me?"

"I hadn't thought about that." He lied. He wasn't about to tell her that he'd intended to drug her, place her in the bath, and slit her wrists.

She laughed. "Wow, you were just going to play along or what?"

"There are ways of killing you that wouldn't come from an overdose, or a beating, or a mugging. Besides, I have no intention of killing you … now." He didn't need her thinking stuff that wasn't the truth.

Kneeling down on the floor, he lifted up her skirt and touched her ankle. He'd noticed she was favoring one instead of the other. Running his fingers around her ankle, he heard her wince. If it was broken, she wouldn't be able to stand on it, so he knew without a doubt that it was sprained. Opening up her sneaker, he slowly eased it off and tossed it aside. "You need to take a shower, and get out of these clothes. If you were on the run, why did you use your own name?" he asked.

She shrugged. "I didn't know he was chasing after me. I didn't want to be at home where he was hurting me. I want him to be thrown in jail, and the key tossed into the ocean or something. He killed my mother. Ever since he came into her life, her health declined for no reason. There was a lot more I've seen. I just know he did it."

Viper released her other sneaker, and tossed that aside. He stood up and pulled off his shirt. "First of all, princess, no one is investigating your mother's death. It was completely natural. You don't know that he killed her."

"For your information, I caught him feeding her bleach. I watched him do it, and when I tried to stop him, he said no one would believe me. Why are you getting undressed?"

"You need to shower. It's getting late. Food and sleep are what I have in mind. You can't stand on that foot, and right now, I don't really trust you. I have this feeling that you're going to be on some kind of mission to get your stepfather thrown in jail. Just a word of warning, everyone is out looking for you, not him."

"I want him to suffer," she said. "He took everything from me."

He helped her down off the counter, and began to pull up her dress. She fisted the fabric, and shook her head.

"You want to stink?" he asked.

"No one has seen me naked before."

Her cheeks were a beautiful shade of red, and he smiled. "I've vowed to take care of you, so you've got nothing to hide from me."

She fought him for another few seconds, and then finally gave up. He liked that she still had that fight inside her. For her to survive he needed to work on her desire to live. He'd already seen up close and personal how she viewed herself, and he found it sad. She was a beautiful woman that believed she wasn't.

It hurt him to see how much belief she had that she was a horrible, ugly person, and that simply wasn't the case. When he looked at her, he only saw beauty, and a strong spirit. She had been hurt, but deep down inside she was a fighter.

"But I'll be naked."

"So will I. We'll both be naked together." He pulled her dress up over her head, and let it fall to the floor. There was some bruising on her ribs, and he assessed the damage. She'd been really lucky. There was nothing broken, but it would hurt for a few weeks. "You're going to be fine."

"How are you going to keep me alive?" she asked. "He's hired so many people to kill me."

"Boss will be taking care of it. Right now, you're with me, and that's your best way to stay alive." He reached behind her and unsnapped the clasp of her bra. Those glorious breasts sprang free. More than anything he wanted to cup those big tits, but instead, he knelt at her feet, and helped remove her panties.

The fine hairs on her pussy were so light that it looked almost bare. He wanted to taste her, and to have those tears changing to cries of pleasure.

Not yet.

He turned on the shower, waiting for the water to run warm.

Then, picking her up, he carried her to the stall, easing her inside. She winced when she put pressure on her foot. He hated seeing her in pain.

"Hold onto me," he said.

"It's fine. I'll be fine."

"I'm going to help you whether you like it or not. Hold onto me now." He held onto her waist.

She placed her hands on his shoulders, and he loved it. He loved her soft curves. Compared to him she was softness and light. For once in his life, he wanted to experience that same kind of feeling, to be soft.

"This is really weird," she said.

"What is?"

"You're the first guy that has seen me naked, and I don't know if I should be embarrassed or not because you've left your jeans on."

He smiled. "That's easily dealt with." Within seconds he was naked. He'd kept his jeans on as he didn't want her to be embarrassed by his very happy state of being with her. His cock was long and thick. "This is what you do to me. I was hoping to save you any discomfort, but I am very happy to be naked with you in the shower."

She gasped, and he chuckled.

Her gaze went to his face. "But I'm fat."

"I think you're beautiful, and I'm starting to think that fleshy ass of yours needs a good spank. Stop calling yourself shitty names. It's not very attractive."

****

Pepper couldn't believe she was standing in the shower with a man, and he had an erection. His cock was so close that he nearly grazed her stomach with the tip. The pain in her ankle didn't help her to focus on something else besides his cock.

This man was a killer. She had to remember that.

Every time she was in his arms though she felt safe.

He protected her, even against that woman back at the shitty hotel.

"Do you bring all the people you need to save here?" she asked.

"No. This is my place. You're the first person here."

"What about when, you know, you want a woman for the night? Are you married?" Crap, what if he had a girlfriend?

"I don't have anyone. All I need is a hard wall when I want a fuck. There are whores, high class and low class, for that."

"Oh."

"Don't worry. I'm clean, and I don't have any diseases. I wear a condom, and after any moment of weakness, I get tested."

"So you get hard for any woman?" she asked.

He spun her around, facing the wall. He placed her hands on the tile, and she watched as he reached for the soap.

"You think my dick is hard just because you're a woman?"

"I—"

"Don't start, I don't want to hear this crap. My dick is hard because I find you very attractive, and if you must know, Pepper, right now, I want to put my dick inside your pussy, and claim that little cherry for my own." She gasped as his hands landed on her stomach. His hands were covered in soap, and she moaned as he began to stroke her body. "These tits, for instance." He cupped them with his fingers. "They're so big, and I just want to see them as you fuck me, see them sway, begging to be sucked. You have large nipples, and I love it when my woman is on the bigger side so I've got something to hold onto. I grab these tits as I fuck you hard." He then pressed her breasts together. "Let's also think about how good it would be to have my dick sliding right here, with your tongue licking the tip." He released a groan. "Damn, one day soon I'm going to see how good that looks."

She couldn't believe that she was even listening to this. It was insane, totally, completely insane, yet she couldn't pull away, nor did she want to. She had known this man a matter of hours, and yet she was attracted to him.

He let go of her breasts and moved his hands down her stomach, going between her thighs. She cried out as he touched her pussy. His finger slid between her slit, and when she attempted to let go of the tiled wall, he ordered her not to. She couldn't resist him, even if she wanted to.

His hands on her body felt so right, and she didn't want him to stop. Not at all.

"You're wet, Pepper." His lips grazed her neck, and she closed her eyes, loving the way he touched her. "Don't worry, I won't pop that little cherry yet, but you and I both know it's only a matter of time before that becomes mine." The hand on her hip left her body, and with the sounds coming from him, he was playing with his cock at the same time he pleasured her.

Two fingers stroked over her clit.

"No man has ever touched you here?" he asked. She shook her head. "No."

"Good. No man will ever touch you but me. This body, you, it now all belongs to me." He sucked on the pulse at her neck, creating so much sensation. "You're so close, aren't you, baby? So close to making yourself come all over my fingers."

"Viper?" She didn't know what was happening to her or how to control it. She was a little scared, and totally enthralled by his power.

"Come for me, Pepper. You won't be judged by me. You need it, and you want it. Let yourself go. Enjoy it."

She fisted her hands on the wall, and cried out his name as the pleasure hurtled into an orgasm that she had never felt before. There had been many nights where she touched herself, hoping to find that peak she had read about, only to forever be evaded by it. This was like something else entirely. For a few short seconds, she was taken completely out of her own head, where nothing mattered.

Behind her, she heard Viper grunt, and something warm landed on her back, and neither of them could speak for several seconds. The pleasure slowly began to fade. Pepper didn't know what to expect. She didn't feel guilty, just happy. Water cascaded around them, and Viper pressed a kiss to her shoulder.

"You sound beautiful when you come," he said.

"Is that what you just did?" she asked.

"Yeah. You didn't for a second think that I wouldn't take something for myself?"

She chuckled. "You're a man that takes what he wants."

"I am, and right now, I want food." He turned the shower off, and it was like reality set in. This wasn't a man she had met on normal terms. He was a man she had hired to help save her.

"Do you think you would have killed me?" she asked.

She held onto the wall as he left the shower, taking a towel. He dried his scarred and heavily inked body. Never did she think she would fall for such a rough man, and yet, she couldn't think of anyone else. The boys she grew up with were always pretending to be men. She couldn't stand them for longer than a few minutes at a time.

"We'll never know." He held the towel against her body, and before she could protest, he was already drying her. She noticed that he kept most of the weight off her foot, and for that, she was grateful. "Are you hungry?"

In answer, her stomach growled.

He chuckled. "I'll get some food going." He lifted her up and carried her through to his bedroom where he placed her on the bed.

Within seconds he had on a pair of sweatpants, and handed her a shirt, and a pair of boxer briefs. He helped her change before they went to his kitchen.

"I can help," she said when he dumped her in a chair at the counter.

"Your ankle must be hurting you. I can cook. I've been doing it for a long time."

"Will you tell me something about yourself?" she asked, curious about this man who had saved her, fingered her, and might have in fact killed her.

"What do you want to know?"

"How long have you been like this?" she asked. She ran fingers through her hair, trying to get rid of some of the knots.

Viper paused, and glanced back at her. "Always."

"Always? What does your family think of that?"

With each word she spoke, he grew tense, the hard line of his back, ramrod straight.

"I didn't have any family. This is the life I have always known, and one that you can never escape from. What about you? What is your family like?" he asked.

"Oh, well, it was fun. Unlike some kids, I didn't get shipped off to boarding school. I went to a private school instead, which was still really scary now that I think about it. Rich kids school I think some people call it. You don't have any family?"

Viper closed the fridge and turned toward her. He was about to speak when his cell phone went off. He picked up the cell, turning on the speaker on so that she could hear the conversation.

"I take it you're at your safe place?" Boss asked.

She recognized the voice.

"We're safe, and she's alive. She's bruised, and in a little pain, but other than that, her injuries are not life threatening," Viper said.

Her cheeks heated as he looked over at her body. She remembered the feel of his fingers on her pussy in the shower.

"Good. It would seem her bone-head stepfather put out a worldwide bounty."

Viper cursed.

"What does that mean?" she asked.

"It means, sweetheart, that unless we kill him, you're never going to know a moment's peace."

"I want him arrested and thrown in jail," she said.

"That's not how this works. He's alive, the bounty exists, and there's always a chance to pay up."

"But he can't pay," she said.

"That's the thing, some people don't mind getting the deed done, and then collecting the bounty after the fact, Pepper. Your life for their money. It depends on what he has offered, how much he has offered, and what they have been promised."

She sat back in the chair, shocked.

"For Pepper to go back to her way of life, we've got to kill him," Viper said, finally speaking up.

"Yeah, otherwise they won't stop coming, and, Pepper, you're going to live the rest of your life waiting to die," Boss said.

"I don't want that," she said.

"Then we kill her stepfather."

Chapter Six

It felt good being on his own territory and not having to look over his shoulder every second. But after three days of lock-down, they were both getting squirrely. It had taken a herculean effort for him to keep his hands to himself, too. He'd been sleeping on the sofa, when he wanted to be in bed with Pepper. It wasn't easy living with her after he'd seen her naked, and made her come on his fingers. She was so eager and receptive. So fucking soft. Normally he wouldn't put his needs to the side, but she was different. She was his. Knowing she'd never been with another man only made his claim stronger.

The sun dipped low on the horizon, the sky morphing into shades of orange and pink. He noticed Pepper standing near the floor to ceiling window in the living room. It was ironic that he lived so high up, only a layer of glass separating him from the massive drop below, because he'd never liked heights. People who knew him swore he was fearless, but he had that one phobia, one he kept to himself.

"How you feeling today?" he asked.

Pepper shifted her head to the side, wearing his oversized t-shirt that nearly reached her knees. "I'm not as sore today. Time really does heal."

"Not everything." He stood beside her, watching the splash of color reflect off the city skyline. Soon only streetlights would keep away the darkness.

"You never did tell me how you got your scar," she said. Pepper faced him and traced her finger along the nasty scar on his face. He'd been a monster for as long as he could remember. Good thing he didn't give a fuck about impressing anyone.

His first instinct was to push her away, but he held back and stood rigid. Talking about his past wasn't a possibility. It was something he tried to forget all his life, and failed. Reliving some of the worst memories would only strip down his barriers.

"You're right, I didn't."

She let her fingers slip away, and she let out an exaggerated breath. "Why can't you talk to me? I mean, *really* talk to me?"

"Some things are better left forgotten."

"It's a simple question," she said. "I'm trying to get to know you better. Every time I think we're having a breakthrough, you pull away. Why?"

"Pepper, don't push this."

She frowned and crossed her arms. The girl was stubborn as a mule. "So, what, you're using me for my inheritance? Is that all you care about, the almighty dollar?"

Viper scoffed. "Look around you, sweetheart, do I look like I need your money?"

"I guess hitmen only know how to use women. No sense actually opening up and getting close, right?" Her sarcasm wasn't lost on him.

He held both her upper arms, securing her in front of him. The sky had darkened since the sun disappeared on the horizon, leaving them in partial shadows. "I haven't had an easy life. Most of it would give a girl like you nightmares, and I'm trying to protect you from that shit. I've never cared about anyone before—until you."

She swallowed hard, her anger draining away. "Then stop putting up walls, Viper."

They sat on his oversized sofa, the one set up with his sheets and pillows. "If you have to know about the damn scar, I'll tell you. When I was a kid, around ten, I think, a pregnant dog got into our compound. We were surprised when they let us keep her. A month later she had five puppies, black with white spots. I can still remember them like it was yesterday."

"That's so sweet."

He frowned. "Six months later they brought us to the main yard. One of the leaders had gathered up the mother dog and pups. He forced us to slaughter them. It had all been a test, to teach us to block out emotion, and remind us that love made us weak."

Pepper cupped her hands over her nose and mouth. "Oh my God, did he cut you for crying?"

"I didn't cry. Didn't even flinch. I knew better."

"Then how did you get the scar?"

"They'd forgotten one of the pups. I hid him in my hut and tried to keep him safe, but as he grew, he wanted to play and I couldn't keep him quiet. When they found out what I did, they beat me, forced me to watch them stomp the life from the puppy, and then used a machete to slice my face."

"Why would they do that?"

"As a warning to the other boys not to break the rules. A visible reminder."

Those assholes had destroyed him, body and soul. But Viper was a man now, and he'd never be a victim again. He bolted to his feet and began to pace, not wanting Pepper's sympathy.

"Where are those wicked men now?"

"They're dead. All of them."

"Oh. How did they die?" she asked.

"I killed them."

It had been a long time coming. It wasn't until he'd physically matured, after the years of training behind him, that he dared to fight back. They'd transformed him into a vicious animal without considering the long-term consequences. It still gave him a natural high when he reflected on that day, the day he took his revenge and snuffed out their evil lives. He'd been killing ever since.

He expected Pepper to turn away in distaste, to judge him, to hate him. It wasn't easy sharing such dark secrets. Instead, she stood up and wrapped her arms around his waist, hugging him. "I'm so sorry," she said. "I can't even imagine living like that. No child should have to go through what you went through."

"Now you know," he said, trying to replicate disinterest.

Her head was pressed to his bare chest. He draped his arms loosely around her. When she started to kiss his pecs, slowly, sensually, his emotions shifted to lust. Passion was ripe in the air, feeding into their mutual desire.

"Pepper, don't start something you can't finish. I've already told you that you belong to me, so I can only hold back for so long."

"Maybe I don't want you to hold back."

If anyone was using a person, it was her. There was no way a good girl like Pepper wanted more than a fling with a man like Viper. She was right, for course— she deserved more; she deserved a man who wasn't broken. But he wouldn't deny her, not when he was pent up and hadn't stopped replaying her little moans from their shower together.

"Take off your shirt," he said. "I want to see your tits."

She actually didn't argue, tugging the shirt off over her head and tossing it on the sofa. Fuck, she looked good enough to eat, all soft curves and milky flesh. Pepper was youth and innocence personified. And he had to claim her, even though he knew he didn't deserve her.

"You're not shy anymore?"

Pepper shook her head. "You're the first man to make me feel beautiful in my own skin. I hope you weren't lying."

He rubbed his rock-hard erection pressing diagonally behind his jogging pants. "I don't need to lie. If I didn't want you, I wouldn't have let you put your hands on me."

"Do you want me now?"

Viper growled, tugging her against his body. He'd never taken a virgin before, and for the past few days he hadn't thought of much else. "No more waiting, baby girl. Tonight I make you mine." He scooped her up into the cradle of his arms, and she let out a cute little squeal. The condo was dark now, only the lights of the city casting their glow through the many windows. He kicked open his bedroom door, and dropped her on the bed.

"I'll get protection," he said.

She shook her head. "I'm on the pill for my periods. I want to feel you. The real you."

He stared down at her naked body, her chest rising and falling in deep, rapid waves. Her blonde hair fanned out over his navy sheets, and her feminine scent had taken over his room. There was uncertainty in her eyes, but also trust. He liked that.

"It's going to be long night," he warned. Viper licked his lips, not sure where he'd start first, but knowing he wouldn't stop until Pepper screamed his name.

****

Pepper stared up at the hulk of a man looming over her. He was a bad boy, hardcore, and dangerous. The man was a killer for hire. But she felt safe, and a little bit in love. She could empathize with him now that she'd been given a glimpse of his past. Everyone had a story, and his explained a lot.

She studied all his dark tattoos, the hard ridges of his muscles, and the intensity in his eyes. Every place he looked, burned with need. Pepper was close to begging, but bit her tongue and waited anxiously for his touch. And, she hoped, his kiss.

He braced one hand on the bed, the mattress sinking. With the other, he painted a line from her ankle to her hip. Then he brushed the backs of his fingers back down along her inner thigh, making her tremble.

"You're so beautiful," he whispered as if mesmerized by the sight of her. Pepper never expected to find a man who would actually appreciate her rather than tolerate her. It was empowering and healing.

He shifted slightly, supporting an arm on either side of her. Viper leaned down and nuzzled her neck, breathing in deeply and releasing a near-growl. Why wasn't he taking what he wanted? How could a killer be so controlled?

Pepper reached up and smoothed her hands over his powerful shoulders. "You have so many tattoos," she said. She never wanted to stop feeling him, savoring the warmth and firmness of his muscles. "Do they mean anything?"

He trailed his lips along her collarbone, a feather light caress. Her nipples were hard and achy, but he never touched her where she needed him most. He was driving her crazy.

"Just old demons. Better on my skin than inside messing with my head."

Viper crawled lower, kissing along her center, making her quiver with need. When he reached the apex of her thighs, she tensed. "Relax, baby. You're mine, so I'm going to enjoy every inch of you."

He spread her legs apart, leaving her so exposed. She felt the cool air swirl against her folds. When he swiped his tongue along her pussy, she cried out and grasped the sheets on either side of her. She'd never felt anything so electric in her life. Viper delved in, licking and sucking as he held her knees open. He sounded like an animal, completely focused on her cunt. "God, you're fucking sweet, baby girl. Soft and sweet and perfect." His voice was a deep baritone, a man on the edge. He flicked her hyper-sensitive bud with his tongue, over and over, making her buck her hips. How could any man be this talented? She closed her eyes, spiraling out of control, barely able to handle the intense pressure building inside of her.

"Viper, I can't take any more!"

He gave her no reprieve, fucking her with his tongue, feasting on her pussy like a starved man. When she thought she'd die from the intensity, she reached a new plateau where everything felt delicious, each pleasure magnified. Pepper's heart raced, and she knew she wouldn't last long. She remembered the shower, and knew this orgasm would win hands down. But before she could explode, he pulled back.

Viper was massive as he rose up, his shadow swallowing her whole. His chest heaved, and his eyes looked feral like wolf spotting its prey. It turned her on even more. She'd never be satisfied with a good boy, not after Viper.

"Why'd you stop?" she managed to ask. He'd stolen that beautiful orgasm away. She wanted it back, needed the relief more than breath.

"I want you to come around my cock," he said, kicking off his jogging pants.

Pepper stared at his erect cock. It jutted out, massive and heavy, dark and ribbed. Would it even fit inside of her? She was anxious but also ever so turned on. "You're big."

He smirked. "Don't think you can handle me?"

"I don't care. Just give it to me."

One of his eyebrows rose. "Bossy little thing, aren't you?" He rested a hand by each side of her head, using the strength in his arms to lower enough to tease her nipples. Pepper let out a moan as he suckled the tight bundles of nerves. "I love these tits."

Viper made her feel sexy to the point she began to love her own body for the first time. It had always been her enemy, but not anymore.

"Kiss me," she said. Pepper wanted to experience full intimacy with Viper. She wanted it all.

He braced himself on his forearms, his hard cock tight to her hip. Why was he looking at her like that? He had a rough five o'clock shadow and thick, kissable lips. Those same lips had just been between her legs, and the mere thought made her clit throb. Their naked bodies were pressed together, and she was only minutes away from losing her virginity. Her core felt like molten lava, and the longer he stalled, the more desperate she became.

"You're going to destroy me." Viper tilted his head slightly, then gave in to her request. He kissed her, a gentle brush at first. Then he really kissed her, their tongues intertwining. It felt so right. She closed her eyes and wrapped her arms around his neck. They devoured each other, no doubts, no holding back.

She wanted to blurt out that she loved him, but wasn't sure if it was her heart or hormones reacting. Viper used his thigh to part her legs, not breaking their kiss. When he ran the thick head of his cock up and down her slick pussy lips, she thought she'd come on the spot. He felt so good, that thick mushroom head promising intense satisfaction to come.

He pushed inside her, the first inch burning as it filled her. She could barely breathe, her nerves and desires bombarding her. Viper tongued the rim of her ear, before sucking on her pulse point. "Good girl," he said.

"Just relax for me. I'll take care of you." For a man who claimed to put his own needs first, he went impossibly slow, easing his big dick into her pussy. She'd never been so wet and achy. He slid inside, inch after thick inch. Once he was fully seated, he exhaled in a groan. "Fuck, you're tight. I never knew a woman could feel this damn good."

Pepper wanted to be everything for him. They were joined together in the most intimate way, her innocence lost, and for some reason it felt so much more than sex. It felt like a physical and emotional bonding, and she prayed he didn't walk away like he had so easily with other women.

Viper began to pump his hips, a slow, steady rhythm at first. He didn't stop, fucking her over and over until the friction brought her orgasm dangerously close to the surface again. Viper was so well-endowed, filling her to overflowing. She wrapped her legs around his waist, prodding him with her heels.

"Behave," he warned, but she didn't care. She wanted him to stop holding back, to fuck her hard and rough like she knew he was capable of. "I don't want to hurt you."

"I can handle it," she said. "I'm a big girl."

He growled. "You're my dirty girl. And I'm going to fuck you real good." He kissed her hard on the mouth as he kicked things up a degree. The bed began to shudder and creak, each thrust making her cry out with pleasure. His back became slick with clean sweat as he tirelessly pumped his hips, pistoning in and out of her hungry cunt. She knew he was close, his movements faster and less erratic. The man was a machine.

Pepper combed her fingers into his hair, pulling his head down, anything to anchor her.

"Come for me," he said. It sounded like a

command, the dominant tone in his voice enough to push her to that perfect place of pre-orgasmic bliss. She panted, a cascade of heat and white light raining down on her. It took one more hard thrust to set her off, her entire body convulsing as wave after wave of contractions rocked her body. Pepper screamed Viper's name, over and over like a mantra.

Then he joined her, his hot seed filling her as he reached his peak. His weight momentarily dropped over her, stealing her breath, until he rolled to the side. "That was better than I imagined," he said. Viper tucked her into the crook of his arm, absently brushing her hair with his fingertips.

Only the sound of their heavy breathing broke the silence in the condo. This was nice. She felt sated like she never thought possible, she felt safe, she felt wanted. If only this moment could last forever.

"You're *my* girl now," he said. "Only mine."

She twisted in his embrace, and began tracing the shape of his chest with a fingertip. "What does that mean, Viper?"

"It means no other man will enjoy your body but me."

"Is that what this is? Just sex?"

He exhaled. "I'm not good at this, sweetheart. Relationships are new for me. I'm trying my best here."

"I just don't want to get hurt," she said.

"I won't kill you, even if Killer of Kings orders it. I can promise you that much."

Pepper didn't want to talk anymore because she was afraid of getting answers she didn't want to hear. She wanted him to tell her he loved her, that he'd never leave her behind. Pepper craved security after enduring the past few months from hell. But now that the lust had settled, she doubted a checkered man like Viper was capable of giving her forever.

"You hungry?" he asked.

She nodded.

"Do you like pizza?"

Pepper loved pizza, and it sounded amazing since they'd been living off Viper's stocked pantry for the past few days. She'd had her fill of canned goods and pasta. "How? Are you getting delivery?"

"No, I'll go pick one up. There's a good place on this block." He slipped out of bed and started getting dressed, tugging on a pair of blue jeans and a long-sleeved black shirt. God, he looked tempting. "Listen to me, Pepper, I don't want you answering the door under any circumstance. Got it?"

"Okay."

"As long as you're here, you're safe. I won't be long."

She looked forward to a night of cuddling with Viper on the sofa, watching movies, and eating pizza. Before he left the room, his cell dinged from a text message. He glanced at the screen for a just a second, then cursed, tossing it on his dresser.

Once she'd heard him leave the condo, the door secured behind him, she got out of bed and stretched. Her body was pleasantly sore. Pepper opened one of Viper's drawers and grabbed a t-shirt. She wandered around. It was strange being alone in Viper's private domain. But there really wasn't anything personal to find because he had no mementos, no pictures, nothing tying him to real life. His phone dinged again, so she checked it out, reading the screen before it faded away. She slapped her hand over her mouth. *Oh no, please no…*

The text was from someone named Maurice. It was a warning. Some Bianchi crime family had put a hit out on Viper for killing one of their men. They were scouring the city. He was in danger.

Pepper danced around the room in a panic. She couldn't call him because he'd left the phone behind. But he'd read the damn message. Did he have a death wish? Or had the first message been something else? She rummaged through her possessions and slipped on her tights. The pizza place was close, so she'd find him, and warn him. Faced with the possibility of losing him, made her realize how much she needed him.

She unbolted the door and ran down the hallway to the elevator, tapping her foot impatiently as she waited. It was late, so she couldn't stop imagining a bunch of paid hitmen ganging up on Viper.

When she reached the ground floor, she rushed out into the street. She didn't care that she looked like shit, her mind only on finding Viper. As she wandered back and forth, wondering which way she should try first, she noticed two black SUVs parked in front of the condo. When she looked closer, the men inside were staring at her with recognition in their eyes. A shiver of fear ran down her spine as she realized how much danger she'd put herself in.

If anyone could handle himself, it was Viper, a trained mercenary with a track record of clean kills. But Pepper was only twenty years old, trapped on the street with no way to get back into the safe haven upstairs, and a worldwide hit on her head.

Chapter Seven

Viper stood in the pizza place. With his order already placed, he looked through one of the menus on the counter. He'd ordered three styles of pizza: pepperoni, spicy meat, and one with anchovies. He didn't like anchovies, but maybe Pepper did. If not, then he could just remove them, and eat it himself.

With his hand in his pocket, he glanced outside of the pizza place, and knew without a doubt that he was being watched. All of his life he'd been trained. If Pepper thought the story he told her about the pups was bad, she didn't even know the half of it. That wasn't so bad compared to the other shit he went through. The people who owned him would make all the kids stand in line, and anyone who failed a task was beaten by another child.

No!

He wasn't going to think about that shit again. The moment he could, he got out. He'd learned to fight back, and he killed every single one of those motherfuckers. Boss had also helped, and that was how he and Boss had become acquainted. That man was a machine and had one of the highest kill ratios in the world.

"Sir, your pizza is ready."

"Thank you."

He looked out of the window and saw the man all dressed in black. This wasn't a kill from Pepper's stepfather. This was something else.

Moving back to the counter, he smiled at the man. "My wife has been nagging me for weeks. You know the pizza wheel thing you guys use, I don't suppose I can buy one from you guys? It'll save me a big headache." He held out a hundred, and the guy was more than happy to oblige.

"Thank you. You're a life saver," Viper said, winking at him.

Leaving the shop, Viper walked down the street aware of the man following him. By his side, out of everyone's line of sight, he held the pizza wheel. This wasn't the most threatening tool to have, but for Viper, it was all he needed.

In the reflection of the shop windows, he saw the man getting close. He made a right turn, placed the pizza boxes on top of a garbage can, and counted to three. As soon as he rounded the corner, he grabbed the stranger, slamming his head against the brick wall. Viper caught him around the throat, and pressed the wheel right next to his artery. With enough pressure to cut the artery, and make the man bleed, it would bring death within seconds.

"Who do you work for?" Viper asked, growling the words.

The man was dazed and didn't answer right away.

Releasing him, Viper picked up the man's gun, pressing the barrel against his head.

"Who do you work for? I'm only going to ask this last time."

"Bianchi, that's the name. You killed one of their guys, and now you've got a big target on your head."

"That's not good," Viper said. The gun would make too much noise. Back to the pizza wheel, he sliced the man's throat, waiting for him to drop. Pocketing the pizza wheel, he grabbed the pizzas, and left the dead man in a heap in the alleyway.

He whistled as he started to walk back toward his place. When he saw Pepper running toward him, he tensed up. What he didn't like was the SUV following behind her.

"What the fuck are you doing out of my

apartment?" he asked, grabbing her arm, and pressing her up behind him, protecting her.

The SUV came to a stop across the street. It was a pretty busy stretch of road, with people passing. No place to have a gunfight and not get attention. He passed Pepper the pizzas and returned to the body only feet away in the alleyway. Bending down, he touched the hips of the guy that he had just killed, and found a knife. The guy must have been pretty good to have come with both items, a gun and a knife. The people who stole him as a child taught them how to make everything at their disposal a weapon. A weak person was the kind that couldn't kill at a moment's notice. Viper wasn't weak.

"Stay here," he said.

He walked over toward the SUV, smashed the window in, and plunged the blade into the first man, and holding his gun out, he aimed it at the second. "I suggest, if you want to live for the next few moments, you step on that gas and call a guy named Boss. Whatever you think you're looking at here, she's not the answer."

The man wasn't a pro. Anyone who came in an SUV didn't know what the fuck they were doing.

Viper stepped back, and watched as the men drove away.

It was a close call.

This shit with Pepper was getting dangerous. Looking back in the alley, he didn't know what that guy's deal was, but they needed to get off the street and fast. He had no doubt that fucking SUV was going to come back. The only way they were safe were back at his place.

"You want to tell me why you're not at my fucking place?" he asked, angered beyond anything.

"Are you like completely insane?" She held his cell phone. The one that had received a text message—the one he couldn't read because that was his biggest secret. He couldn't fucking read. Pepper was behaving as if a few moments ago men weren't intent on taking her and killing her. She was so close to having gotten killed.

This was one of the reasons why he didn't fuck on the job. It always ended up getting someone killed.

Gritting his teeth, he held onto her arm, and marched her all the way back to his apartment, dealing with each of the codes that was necessary before they were secure.

"Stop it, Viper. Please listen to me."

"Do you have any fucking idea how many people want you dead? Those men in the SUV were not even fucking trained. They were just a bunch of wannabes, and you think I want to listen to you? I told you to stay fucking here!" he yelled. Viper grabbed the pizzas, shoving them under one arm before pushing her against the elevator that would take them up to the main floor of his home.

"People want you dead as well, so guess what? We're both up shit creek. I saw those guys, and I ran, okay? I made sure I got somewhere that they couldn't take me. They were a little shocked that I did it. I got away, no big deal."

Viper just stared at her, teeth gritted. "You and I are not alike. What you got today was fucking lucky."

"I know that. You went out even though there's a massive bounty on your head. Check your cell phone. Go on, check it. See for yourself. You looked at your cell before leaving. Why did you go out? Pizza doesn't mean anything to me, Viper. We could have made something from the stuff in your kitchen."

She held the cell phone up, and all he saw was Maurice's name. That was it. He'd intended to give his friend, correction, associate a call to make sure he was okay.

"You shouldn't have been outside." He released her arm, and she gasped, making him look back down. There was blood on her arm.

"Viper, you're bleeding."

"It's not my blood." Even as he spoke, she grabbed his hand, holding it out. "See, no cut. It's not my cut, and the difference between the two of us is the fact I know how to handle myself. You had no consideration at all for the fact that you could have been watched." The elevator doors pinged open, and he stepped inside.

The happy zone he'd been in moments ago had vanished, and now he was fucking pissed. He went to the bathroom sink, and washed off the blood that he'd gotten onto his hand, tossing the pizza wheel in the sink as well.

"Viper," Pepper said, standing near to him. She held the phone out. "Read the text."

"I don't need to read that shit. I was prepared, okay?"

"That pizza wheel is covered in blood. You had no idea of that threat or you would have taken your guns."

Viper moved away from the sink, dried his hands on a towel, and grabbed a slice of pizza. "Are you going to eat?"

Pepper washed the blood off her arm, and then turned to look at him. He didn't like the way she was assessing him.

"Eat some pizza. Do you like anchovies?" he asked.

"I hate them," she said. "Back in the hotel room, you asked me to read you something. And on the cell phone, you told Boss not to text you." She tilted her head to the side, and stared at him. "You were taken as a child, tortured, trained to kill."

"Again with the whole information dump. As

fascinating as this is, I'm bored."

"You can't read, can you?" she asked.

Viper took a bite of the pizza and stared at her. He didn't tell anyone that secret. Boss didn't even know. As far as Boss was concerned, Viper was an asshole for demanding vocal instructions. He didn't give a shit what anyone thought of him. Maurice didn't know, and the bastards who kept him as a kid made sure their killing machines did as they were told. They were not taught or allowed to read. He knew numbers, and that was all.

"What are you staring at?" he asked.

Tears flooded her eyes, and she shook her head. "Wow, you're going to be an asshole, is that it?"

"Babe, I don't know what you're thinking right now, but you're paying me to keep you alive, and that's what I'm doing. I'm keeping you alive. You got a problem with that?"

She shook her head. "No, I don't have a problem with that." Pepper stormed away, and he cursed himself.

"Pepper, you've got to eat."

"What I don't need right now is to be around an asshole like you. That's what I don't want!" She slammed his bedroom door closed, and he tossed the pizza in the trash. He was no longer hungry. How the fuck did she figure that shit out from one text?

He'd kept this secret for a long fucking time. No one knew.

Tapping his hand on the counter, he was about to go and see Pepper when his cell phone rang.

"What?" he asked.

"Mind the attitude. Bianchi has put a hit out on you."

"I was out to get pizza and found a guy lurking. He's dead so there's no reason to worry at all. What I didn't like was the fact there was an SUV scoping my place. I can't stay here. They'll be back."

"You're going to need to move. I've got a safe house set up for you. It's secluded, and you're not going to have to worry about anyone finding it," Boss said.

Viper was intrigued. "Where is it?"

"It's my house."

"Boss, I'm not going to hang out at your place."

"You've got no choice. The bounty on your head is high enough, and Pepper's has just doubled. I'm not about to lose money."

Viper tensed, and Boss tsked.

"I'm not going to fucking kill you, Viper. The money they're offering is not enough."

"How much?" Viper asked.

"Two mill. That's not enough to kill you in my book. I can earn that from you in a few months, and that's exactly what I intend to do. You're a good worker," Boss said.

"Ah, would you miss me if I ended up dead?"

"Don't push your fucking luck."

****

They were back on the road again, the scenery passing her by as they made their way once again to another safe house. Pepper rested her head on her hand refusing to look at the man she had given her virginity to.

Yes, she had been afraid when she saw those guys in the SUV. She knew Viper wouldn't let anything happen to her, and so she had run. The last thing those guys needed was to expose her kidnapping on the television. Being in a public place was the best thing for her. Her stepfather needed her to die of natural causes. Being run down by a car was kind of natural until they investigated. His ass would get thrown in jail, and the money wouldn't go to anyone but charity. The business would be broken down, and sold off piece by piece.

No, her stepfather didn't want that. He wanted control.

"I'm sorry," Viper said.

She turned to find him still staring straight ahead. It was early evening. The sun was still shining in the sky, and they were traveling on a busy road.

Pepper didn't say anything, and instead went back to looking outside.

"Did you hear me?"

"I heard you. I'm choosing not to listen. It's what a woman does best, so I've been told."

She heard him sigh, and refused to help him with this. He had been a total asshole.

"I was worried, okay? It has been a long time since I had a bounty on *my* head. I was unprepared, and I fucked up yesterday. I shouldn't have gotten pizza, and then I saw you running toward me, and I flipped out."

"Yeah, well, normal boyfriends don't have to deal with a band of killers chasing after their girlfriend, do they?" She ran her fingers through her hair, hating every single second of this. "Are we there yet?"

"Still got another thirty minutes. I want to stay in public. It's the only way I'm keeping you safe. How are you feeling?"

"I'm fine!" She snapped the words out, and then regretted it. "I'm sorry. It's been a really shitty day. Actually, you know what, scrap that. It has been a fantastic day that has turned into a crappy one. I'm going from one safe house to another because of some asshole, and now I'm arguing with you. I don't even know why you're angry with me. I asked you a simple question, and you behave like this? You know what? Forget it. Forget I ever said anything. I didn't ask for this. I didn't ask to be killed, or to have my mother murdered. I just wanted to live a normal life, or as close to a normal life as one can get." She was nowhere near done. "You know what? I'm sick and tired of all of this. I was a good person. That asshole who came along destroyed everything. He killed my mom. You know what is even stupider, as I'm sitting here right now all I can think about is how good last night was. I gave my virginity to you, and then you treat me like this. I want to hate you so much."

There, she was done.

Once she realized what she had said, she groaned.

"I don't think stupider is a word," Viper said. He sounded so calm that it had her looking toward him, and yes, he was staring straight ahead at the road. "You can't take my word for it of course. I don't know if there's a word like that in the dictionary." She froze. "You're right, and I hated to admit my weakness to you." He glanced over at her. "I can't read. I've never been able to read."

"No one taught you?"

"The bottom line was money, Pepper. I don't need to know anything but numbers, and that's all I know." She didn't need to know that there had been someone there who had his back. His entire childhood had been one fucked up mess after another, but even when he'd been at his worst, there had been one person who helped him through—Bain. Bain was the only person from his past that he'd any kind of feelings for. They were sworn together as brothers to fight those who had taken them and hurt them. After they had completed their mission by taking out those sick fucks, he'd only seen Bain once or twice throughout the years. Viper rarely thought about him, but there were times he wondered if the bastard was dead.

"How can you take orders?"

"Boss tells me. I have a great memory, and the thing about GPS nowadays, they tell you what to do." He shrugged. "No one knows. You're the first person to figure it out."

"Were you born to that way of life?" she asked.

"What do you mean?"

"You talk about being in some kind of prison. Were you born there?"

She watched as he stared straight ahead. "I don't have any memory of the time before. I know I wasn't born into that way of life. I did some digging. I was stolen from my mom's side when I was three years old."

She covered her mouth, shocked. "You must have been afraid."

"I can't remember. Growing up there was fear. It didn't change, and when I was old enough, I settled the score with those bastards."

Pepper didn't know what to say. "You had no idea that there was a hit out on you?"

"Nope." He said the word with a pop to it.

"You're not afraid?"

"Nope. This won't be the first time I've had a bounty on my head."

"How did you stop the bounty?"

"By killing the person who placed it on my head. It's not easy to do with a target on your back."

"We need to kill my stepfather."

"Yes, we do."

"And we need to kill Bianchi?"

"We do if I want to have a life."

Pepper sat back. "Wait, I can be seen in public, right? My death has to be of natural causes."

"Yeah, I guess."

"Why don't I just go home?"

She saw she had confused him.

"Think about it. I could go home. No one knows where I've been. We can go public, and I can tell them that I had married you." The more she thought about it, the more she liked it.

"Pepper—"

"That company is mine, Viper. Every single part of it. I can just go and take it. I don't need to be on the run. We can kill two birds with one stone."

She watched as he started to tap the steering wheel.

"It'll get us closer to my stepfather."

"How do you say you met me?" he asked.

"Simple. You're my bodyguard. One thing led to another, and we've been locked away on some island off the coast or something. No television, no nothing but our romance. We can make this work. People make this kind of stuff work all of the time." Silence met her plan. Pepper was excited. "The sooner we get to my stepfather, the sooner we can end this. Bianchi wouldn't be able to take you out being in the public eye, right? It would offer you some form of protection, too."

"I'm not good for being broadcast. My scars."

"Everyone loves a bad boy. Come on, Viper, this is a really good idea." She touched his arm, excited to even be thinking about it.

"I'm going to need to run it by Boss first."

Pepper patted her thighs. "How about we phone him now?"

"Just calm down. I want time to think about this."

Once again silence filled the car, and she couldn't take it anymore. After the night they'd had, she didn't want there to be any more silence.

"I think it's a great idea. We can say that I had an argument with my mom, which isn't a lie really. We did argue, and I'd had enough. I couldn't handle the pain that he inflicted on me, so I ran. You followed me, took care of me, and during that time we fell in love, got married."

"I've been consoling you ever since?" he asked.

"Yes, exactly. We can pull this off, right? Wait, we can't get married."

"Boss can get the relevant paperwork, and at a later date we can use a priest if we decide to keep it going."

She liked that. He was planning for a future with her. Or so she hoped. They may not be on the best speaking terms, but she liked this plan a hell of a lot.

The drive to Boss's secret house took far too long for her, but she stayed quiet so that Viper could think.

When they got there, a large hulk of a man was already waiting. He had dark hair that was down to his shoulders, and two scars down his eye.

"Viper," he said.

"Boss. Pepper, this is Boss. Boss, this is Pepper."

"Nice to meet you at last."

He was so big, so scary that it made her swallow. Her heart started to race, and she glanced at Viper, seeing he wasn't afraid.

"I'm not going to hurt you, Pepper," Boss said, opening his gates. He waited for them to enter, and she didn't like having him at her back. She had paid this man ten million dollars to keep her alive. Unless someone else had come up with a higher price, he worked for her. "I thought you had gotten lost."

"No, we weren't lost," Viper said. "Believe it or not, Pepper has a plan. Tell him."

She gritted her teeth hating being put on the spot, and he'd done it on purpose. He didn't really think her plan was a good idea. Licking her dry lips, she began talking at the same time they all started walking toward the main house.

Once she had finished, they were securely inside, and Boss had his arms crossed over his chest, looking deep in thought.

"What do you think?" she asked.

"That could work. I can have the documents here within the hour. Do you know anyone in the media who would do a press release for you?"

"Yes, I do, and I can even have it arranged for outside my family's company."

Boss smiled, and in a weird way that made him look even scarier.

She tensed up waiting, and then he nodded.

"Let's get this party on the road."

Chapter Eight

Viper wasn't sold on Pepper's idea. So many things could go wrong. She was too naive for her own damn good, not realizing how many targets would be on her back once they went public. He didn't want to lose her.

He stood against a far wall in the living room with his arms crossed, watching Pepper explore Boss's vast art collection. His mind was in overdrive as he plotted several murders in his head—and the fact he'd fallen for a mark. He was an idiot. After a lifetime of keeping his guards safely in place, never letting a woman under his skin, Pepper had walked into his life and changed everything. She was too young and innocent for him, but the thought of any other man having her made a deep-seated rage burn inside him. Pepper was his. He'd crossed that line, and there was no turning back now.

He'd never had anything of value as a child, taught not to keep mementos or get attached to anything or anyone. But he'd taken control of his future a long time ago. Pepper would be his prize, the one thing he wouldn't let anyone take from him.

"The way you watch her … shit, Viper." Boss leaned against the wall next to him.

Viper didn't comment.

"Killer of Kings can't have hitmen who fall for their marks. We'd go out of business in no time."

When Viper turned his head to gauge Boss's expression, the bastard winked, a look of amusement on his face.

"This is fun for you?" he asked.

Boss shrugged. "I just feel sorry for the fool who makes a move on that girl." He chuckled.

Viper pushed off from the wall, not comfortable

with topic of conversation, and even more disturbed that he was so transparent. "I'll get the job done. This changes nothing."

"That's where you're wrong, Viper. I've seen it before—love changes everything. One thing's for damn sure, a piece of pussy will never tear down *my* empire. Weren't you the one always telling me women were just a weakness used to exploit us?"

Viper whirled around, running both hands through his hair, tempted to pull in out at the roots. "Are the papers in? I've got to get the fuck out of here."

"Sure," he said. "They came fifteen minutes ago."

Viper felt cornered, bristling like a feral dog. This was the first time in his life he had something worth saving, and it terrified him. Viper watched Pepper trail her finger along one of the larger bronze statues. Everything about her mesmerized him, from the color of her hair to the curves of her body. She turned as if sensing his gaze, giving him a little smile.

"Pepper, come on, it's time to go."

As he started to walk through the marble entrance arch of the room, Boss placed a heavy hand on his shoulder. "One word of advice. If shit gets ugly, save yourself first. We've already been paid in advance. I don't want to lose one of my best men."

He jerked away from Boss, heading straight for the front doors of the mansion. The place was fucking huge, and looked more like an Italian museum than the hideout for a crime kingpin. It was even more secure than Viper's condo. He noticed every little intricacy from the thugs around the property to the state of the art security and surveillance system in every corner.

"Wait up," Pepper called out as she ran through the lobby. "We're already leaving?"

"The marriage documents are ready. There's no

sense sitting around, wasting time. Best to get on the road." His mood had soured. Boss had forced him to examine his feelings and any future with Pepper. Maybe dreaming up a happy ending with her was bullshit for a fuckup like him.

He walked ahead of her, too fast for her to keep up. His eyes were on the Mustang just outside the main gates. His escape. Moving from one job to the next was what he did best. Settling down could never work.

By the time the iron gates began to automatically open with an eerie whine, Boss and a couple of his hired guns had caught up. Viper wasted no time getting into the car, squeezing the steering wheel with both fists like a lifeline. Pepper sat in the passenger seat, and then Boss leaned over and tapped on the driver's side window.

He started up the car, now equipped with a working key, before lowering the tinted glass.

"I had your plates changed, too. The ones you had were hot." Boss stood back up, looking at the dark cloud cover moving in. "Call me when the job is done."

"I always do." Then he hit the gas, reversing out the long winding driveway. That's what he liked: clean, efficient, no bullshit. Why did Boss have to push his buttons today? He usually knew better, but then again, Viper had never shown interest in any of the whores who frequented Boss's place. He'd never cared about any woman.

They'd been driving for a while in silence, awkward silence.

"Is something wrong?" Pepper asked.

"This is a big move we're taking. A lot can go wrong. Your stepfather isn't going to hand everything over without a fight."

"Well, I'm hoping there won't be a fight. Like I said, this plan is perfect. Nothing can go wrong."

Her positivity was cute, but it was all an illusion. The reality was going to be equivalent to a shit storm. "Whatever you say, Pepper."

"It's true. You'll see." She leaned over the center console and rested her head on his arm. He felt his muscles relaxing and breath softening. It was odd having a woman cling to him for safety and affection. She had no idea the power she held over him.

The landscape changed from rural to urban to rural again. In another half hour they'd reach the city. Viper had a bad feeling about showing up unannounced at Pepper's house. His renowned confidence was at an all-time low because this time he had something to lose.

"Kiss me," she said.

He frowned. "Now? I'm driving."

"You're trying to pull away from me. I can feel it. Ever since those texts you've been distant."

"Distant?"

"If you think I feel differently about you because of the reading thing, I don't."

He didn't like where this was going. Pepper was an educated girl from a wealthy family. There was no way she'd be happy with an illiterate man like Viper. His fucking insecurities had shown their ugly colors since Pepper walked into his life. He wished things were different, but they weren't.

"Viper, please say something." She placed her hand on his thigh. "I need you. I don't have anyone else."

He abruptly hit the brakes, parking in an abandoned alcove along the side of the road and cut the engine. "I don't want you to settle, Pepper. You deserve more."

"I'm not settling, so don't put words in my mouth."

"What can I give you?"

"Look, I've known so many Ivy League boys in my life. I don't want them, I want you, a real man. You can take care of me, Viper. In every way."

Fuck, the way she said those last words made his cock swell in his jeans. He twisted uncomfortably in his seat. "You want that kiss or what?"

She smiled and leaned closer. He cupped the side of her face and kissed her hard and demanding. She even tasted sweet. Her little mewling sounds were pushing him over the edge.

As soon as their tongues began to play, he pulled away and left the car, slamming the door behind him.

Pepper rushed out, joining him at the rear of the car. Her little hands were balled into fists, her brow lowered. "What was that about? What did I do wrong now?"

Her grabbed her by the waist and hoisted her up onto the back of the Mustang, pressing himself between her legs. "I need you."

"What?" Her voice was barely a whisper, her hands resting on his shoulders.

He lifted up her shirt with one hand, while fiddling with his belt buckle with the other. Her tits were gorgeous. He quickly realized he was addicted to everything Pepper. He peeled back the cup of her bra and took her areola into his mouth, sucking hard.

"Get your pants off, baby. I want my dick inside you."

She let out a little gasp, but did as she was told, wiggling out of her pants while seated on the trunk of the car. He pulled them clean off once they shifted down her hips. Maybe another time he'd take things slow, savoring her body—not now. They were about to risk their lives with this volatile plan, and Viper had been craving a piece of Pepper since their first encounter. Just remembering the moment he took her virginity was enough to set him off. She'd given him more than her innocence. Her gift made him feel special in a world that had always told him he was nothing more than a shadow.

But right now was about sex. Hard and dirty.

Viper spread her legs wide, tugging her ass until she slid to the very edge of the trunk. He positioned himself, rubbing the ready end of his cock in her overflow of juices.

"Oh God," she said, bracing her hands on either side of her. Her eyes were hooded, her full lips parted.

He pushed inside her until seated to the hilt. She was so tight and hot, her pretty, pink pussy gripping him like a fist. Viper growled, the instant relief after sliding inside her incomparable. "You feel so damn good, baby girl. Tell me you want to be fucked."

"No, I can't say that."

Her body was full of his cock, her shirt rolled up atop her breasts. The odd car zoomed by on the highway, but they were partially hidden in their alcove within the dense forest.

He kissed her, determined to get her to submit. She wrapped her arms around his neck, squirming against his cock, but he refused to give her what she needed.

"Viper, please."

"Say it." He ducked down and licked her tight nipples, flicking them with his tongue.

"I want you … to fuck me," she said.

"Do you want me to make you come?"

"Yes!"

He couldn't hold back his own needs a second longer. Viper grasped her hips and fucked her good, ramming into her lush body with enough stamina to rock the car. He was pent up and hard as steel.

Pepper moaned and squealed, the erotic sounds

drowning out the sounds of nature. He loved how she held onto him, her nails digging unforgivingly into his skin. The pain only spurred him on.

He pumped into her hot cunt over and over, kissing her lips, the rim of her ear, her neck.

"I love you," she said. Then her body erupted, her pussy rhythmically milking his cock. He came in a powerful rush, groaning as he met his own release.

Their breathing was rapid as they relished in the aftermath. Viper stayed in place, their bodies still connected. Had he heard right? It had to be words spoken in the moment of passion. No one had every loved him, certainly not a woman. The longest relationship he'd ever had was three weeks, if he couldn't even call it more than an extended booty call.

Pepper was a good girl. *His girl*.

He took a last deep breath, then lifted her down to her feet so she could get dressed. Viper zipped up and then popped the trunk. He opened his traveling arsenal, displaying the full array of weapons he'd packed up when they left his condo.

"What the hell?" Pepper stared at the guns.

"Get dressed, princess." He buckled on his bun belt and harnesses, then began filling every holster with a lethal weapon. Each one had a silencer, just in case he needed to keep on the down low. By the time he closed the case, he was a one-man killing machine.

Once they were back in the car, he noticed the fear in Pepper's eyes. He didn't like it.

"I'm scared," she said. "I wish this was all a nightmare I could wake up from."

"You know why this has to happen. We have to set things right."

"What if something happens to me?" She looked like pure innocence with those big, blue eyes.

"I won't let anyone hurt you," he said. "You're mine to protect."

****

When her house came into view it was like looking through a portal in time. A wash of emotion took her by surprise. She remembered her mother, but mostly the fear the house represented thanks to her horrible stepfather. Her body felt stiff, her nerves on edge. What was she thinking to go through with this plan? Now that they had arrived, her confidence dwindled.

"Shit, your place is huge."

"Appearances mean nothing," she said. "I could never live in that house again. It only reminds me of his cruelty."

"Bernard Sutherland," Viper recited, a deadly inclination in his tone.

"He's the worst."

"Is that your name? Pepper Sutherland?"

"No! I have my mother's name, Henshaw." There was no way she wanted to be associated with that monster, that murderer.

They pulled around to the side street next to the house. Viper had his leather jacket on, effectively concealing his weapons. He was more on edge than usual, his focus seemingly on everything at once.

"They're not here. I thought you told the media crew to meet you at seven sharp?"

Pepper looked at the dashboard clock, and it was already twenty minutes after. It seemed odd they'd be late for such a breaking news case. As much as she felt safe with Viper, part of her believed she'd meet the same fate as her mother. "I don't understand why they're not here."

Viper scanned the area, his eyes narrowed. "That's because they're dead."

"What!"

He raced the car up the street, way above the inner-city speed limit. The sound of the engine was deafening. Her heart pumped like a freight train, and she had to remind herself just to breathe. Viper stopped in the old alleyway behind her house, mostly used for deliveries and storing the dumpsters.

"Get out," he said.

"Viper, what's happening?"

"Hush now. Keep quiet and do as I say."

She followed behind him, holding the edge of his jacket like a lifeline. He appeared like a man taking a casual stroll on the beach, his shoulders back and each stride strong and confident. He had one hand inside his jacket, and he used his free one to test the back door. It was locked. Viper squatted down after checking around. Within seconds he'd picked the lock.

Once inside the only home she'd ever known, she felt dirty and violated. Her stepfather didn't deserve to take over everything. She noticed little things, like family portraits and small trinkets she'd bought with her mother when she was a child. He'd taken everything from her. Her anger gave her the confidence she desperately needed right now. Even if she never lived here again, there was no way she could stand the thought of her mother's murderer enjoying it.

"Stay here," Viper whispered. "I'm going to check over there."

Pepper didn't like being left alone, but she did as she was told. She kept fiddling with the hem of her shirt hoping he'd come back quickly, but after a while she heard two male voices coming from the other hallway. She froze, a jolt of panic paralyzing her like back at that hotel. She tried to call out for Viper, but her voice didn't work.

"Someone's there," said one of the men. When

they both noticed her, they were quick to pull out guns. God, she hated guns, especially when pointed at *her*.

"It's the fucking girl. I can't believe this. How's that possible?" said the blond.

"Hell if I know. There still a price on her head?"

The blond smirked. "Damn right there is. Sutherland never said we couldn't cash in. Do you remember the terms?"

"Natural causes. That's it."

"It won't look good if she tanks in her own house. Let's drive her out to the suburbs and dump her," said the blond.

Pepper still hadn't moved. She felt like she was having an out of body experience, watching a movie where she had the unfortunate starring role.

They started to move in, cornering her, like hunters approaching a skittish animal. "Hey there, Pepper. Don't be scared. I'm sure your stepdad will be thrilled to see you."

The blond slowly reached out for her arm, but before he could make contact there was a shrill popping sound. He dropped straight backwards like a falling oak, crashing onto the wooden floor. The other guy waved his gun back and forth like a madman looking for a ghost. There was another pop, and a well of blood appeared on his forehead. He stared at her blankly before collapsing into a heap.

"Come on." Viper took her hand and tugged her along. She kept looking back at the two dead bodies, shocked and speechless. He ushered them through two different doors, but she wasn't paying attention.

"Who were they?"

"Don't know. Don't care."

He pressed her against a wall as he cracked open another door. She tried to focus and get her wits back.

They were about to enter the front foyer of the house. She could hear voices, and imagined there would be a lot of security at the entrance. The sun had faded, and there was little light in the corridor. According to Viper her stepfather's hired men had killed the media crew, destroying her entire plan. Instead of laying claim to her fortune, she was a rat in a maze where everyone wanted her dead.

A man with an automatic weapon was waiting on the other side of the door. He aimed at Viper, and Pepper screamed. She watched in horror as several other men rushed over, shouting and brandishing firearms. *What have I done?*

Viper used a Glock with unbelievable accuracy, aiming and shooting, taking them down one by one. More footsteps echoed in the house. He dropped his gun, shrugged off his jacket, and reached into a holster for another weapon.

She crouched down low, watching Viper move about like a one-man killing machine—shooting, punching, and flipping men like a choreographed dance.

He was slightly out of breath when he finally checked on her. "You're doing great, baby. Time to go." Viper helped her up to her feet, but was blindsided by a huge man dressed in black. They crashed into the opposite wall, drywall raining down from the impact. Both men were powerhouses, bare knuckle boxing back and forth with no holding back. Viper was in his fitted t-shirt, strapped with weapons. His muscles were straining, and she prayed he was capable of coming out on top. If anything happened to him, she was as good as dead.

"Fuck," Viper cursed, taking a shot with a gun but missing when the brute knocked his arm to the side. The bullet whizzed near Pepper's head making her squeal.

"Submit, fucker!" The other man used the same

moves, making it impossible for one to overpower the other. This hired gun had a shaved head with dark stubble and tattoos on his neck. She wasn't sure which man looked scarier.

More gunshots fired, and then they were both on the floor, wrestling. Viper got the other man into a head lock, his massive biceps bulging as he applied intense pressure. Within minutes, the man's body went limp, and the house seemed eerily quiet again. Only the sound of Viper's heavy breathing broke the hush.

"Is he dead?" she asked, crawling over to Viper. He had blood coming from his lip and a blackening eye. She wanted to kiss every inch of his face, so relieved he was okay.

Viper shook his head, pushing up into a sitting position. He leaned against the wall. "He's just out cold. I couldn't kill him."

"Why not?" Of all the other hitmen, this guy seemed like the stiffest competition. She didn't want him to wake up and kill her man.

"His name's Bain. He's a ghost from my past."

Chapter Nine

Back at another motel, Viper paced the length of the room right near the front door. The lights were turned off, and as much as he wanted to join Pepper in the shower, he stayed to guard. Now was not the time to be enjoying a nice fuck before bed. He needed to get shit dealt with. It was like thinking about Bain had brought him out of thin fucking air.

"What's the news?" he asked the moment Boss answered the call.

"That the attack on the media has been considered an accident. One of the hitmen dressed as a reporter opened fire, and killed them all. None of them were rolling their cameras, but the security footage on the outside of the building confirms it. As far as law enforcement is concerned, one crazy man whom they can't identify did it. Fucking assholes."

Boss didn't sound impressed, and what concerned Viper was what he sensed was coming next.

"Viper, either Sutherland goes down, or she does. It's one or the other. You can't keep her alive forever."

"I know." He glanced toward the shower.

"Can you do it? Can you kill her? It would end all of this. We have the ten million advance. Kill her, get it over with, and return to your life."

Any mercenary would see the instant they were pushed into a corner. There were too many risks. They had taken out reporters now, and it was only getting worse. "Bain was there."

"What?"

Bain was not only someone from his past, he was also someone that Boss had tried to bring into the fold.

"Yeah, he was there. I couldn't kill him. Look, I know I should just take care of everything, and we'd be up financially, but I can't do it. I can't … kill her. I don't want to." He rubbed at his eyes, feeling the strain of everything. She had admitted that she loved him. It had been during the throes of sex, but those words had meant something to him.

It was stupid, but no one in his entire life had ever told him that they loved him. No one. He'd always been a thing to train for them to get to be a killing machine, and he couldn't kill her, not even if he wanted to.

"I didn't think you'd kill her." Boss sighed on the other end. "She is not going to last much longer, Viper. The kills on her head, I looked into her family's fortune, and it's fucking huge. We're talking an empire forged hundreds of years ago that has only gotten stronger. It has survived so fucking much, and continues to. They employ hundreds of thousands, and they actually have a good work ethic. She's far from a pampered princess."

"You want her to live?" he asked.

"Yeah, I do. She's worth more to us alive than dead and not just because of our paycheck. If Sutherland takes over that company, heads will roll. The man is pure evil, and he's got to die. I've found out the reason he's got so many men on his side. He's offered them a percentage of the company, Viper. That's millions if not billions of dollars."

Viper knew what he had to do. "Tomorrow, I'll go."

"Viper, you've got to use her as bait. I've got the sedative that will make it look like she's dead. The only way you will get close is if you take her with you. This guy is not going to stop, and he's going to have a shitload of men around him."

Again, he was rubbing his eyes. Everything that he had to deal with, he'd handle tomorrow.

"I'm going to need back up, and I want tonight

with her. Give me that, please."

What he was planning would certainly kill the two of them, but he wasn't about to risk either of their lives, not for a second.

"We're guarding you. You have nothing to fear. Have your night, and enjoy it." Boss ended the call, and Viper clicked the phone off, holding it in his hand, and wanting to crush it so it didn't disturb him again. When he turned, he found Pepper sitting on the bed. Even in the dark, he knew she was sad.

"I didn't hear you finish in the bathroom."

"You were talking."

"You heard some of that?"

"Yeah, I heard some of that. You can't kill me, or you don't want to kill me?"

Tears glistened in her eyes, and it twisted his gut to see them. He couldn't handle this, not for a second. It was all too much for him, and he gritted his teeth. Never had he felt such weakness, and yet was it really weak to love a woman? "I'm not very good at this."

"All you have to do is answer the question."

"I can't kill you, okay? Do you know how easy all of this shit would be?" He exploded. He was angry, enraged, and just plain pissed off. Deep down he had known this fucking plan wouldn't work. Sutherland was too much of a greedy bastard to let some woman take from him what he'd been wanting all along, power, money, everything. Her mother had been too fucking weak to see what was going on, and now her own daughter was having to pay the consequences of that. "I could kill you right now, and have the money you've sent as a payment, and then whatever Sutherland will pay. That is how easy I can end this."

"Then do it."

He shook his head and growled. "You're so

infuriating, you know that? You're rich, and have this perfect life, and yet you don't. This is not supposed to happen. Not to me."

"What's not supposed to happen?"

He had confused her. "This! I shouldn't want you, Pepper. I'm a bad guy. All I've ever known is violence. I can't even fucking read, and yet I have a piece of paper in my pocket to say that we're married, and all I want to do is fucking read it, and for it to actually be true. Do you even get that?" He heard her gasp, and yet continued anyway. There was no point in stopping while he was on a roll. "There are men willing to take out a whole group of reporters to see you dead, and to get one big paycheck. A paycheck that I was on the way to get when I first met you."

"Then do it, Viper. I don't want to cause you any more pain." She stood, holding onto the towel. Her hair was still wet, and she looked so pitiful, yet he fucking loved her. This woman, this stupid woman who ran away just to be safe. *Damn it.* "I don't want you to be hurting because of me."

"You stupid, stupid, woman." He reached out, cupping her cheeks. Pressing his head against hers, he tried to calm his rage. "I do not want to, and I will not kill you."

"It will make your life easier."

"A life without you, Pepper, will not make my life easier." He pressed a little kiss to her lips. "I want that wedding certificate to be real, not just on paper, I mean, but for us both to be married. I don't want to kill you because I couldn't live without you." Even as he spoke he was finding it hard to speak the words.

Every single moment growing up, whenever he wanted something, or loved something, it was taken from him. Pepper at any moment could be taken from him, and he couldn't handle that. Her dying just couldn't happen. He refused to allow it.

"I love you, Pepper." He gritted his teeth. "And because I love you, I cannot let you die. I'm going to fight for you, fight for us, and I'm not, no matter what you think, going to let you die. I can't do allow it."

There was silence, and Pepper stared at him, no words coming from her.

"You love me?" She was the first to break that silence.

"Yes."

"You want to marry me?"

"Know a woman to be the first to pick that out."

"I'm being serious, Viper. You want to marry me?" she asked.

"Yes. I want to marry you. I want to belong to you."

"Then we can get married, you know. Before we go and deal with *him*. If anything goes wrong, you can have it all. You'll be the next in line as my husband to inherit my family fortune. I want you to have it."

He pressed a finger to her lips, to silence any more words or plans from her. The last thing he wanted to be talking about right now was what was about to happen. She had no idea that this threat was never going to go away. They only had each other for this one night, and then he was going to have to fight, and to fight hard. "I don't want you to be thinking about that, or about anything else right now, okay?"

"Viper, we can do this together. I know we can."

She always saw the positive, and never what had to happen. It was like she was either blind, or refused to see the truth. He loved that about her. Even after everything, knowing what he did, she never judged him.

"Why couldn't we have met a couple of years

ago?" He wasn't asking her, or anyone else. The truth was, he deeply regretted his life for a split second, and wished there was some way to end it.

He wasn't a good man, never would be. Tilting her head back, he stared into her eyes, and tried to remember everything he loved about the color blue. How it reminded him of the ocean, of the dreams that would often come to him as a boy. Stroking her cheek, he relished the softness of her skin, and then he remembered the feeling of her tight, virgin pussy wrapped around his cock.

For as much as he could be poetic in their last night together, he still was a man, a man with needs. He stared at the knot holding the towel together. Her skin had dried a little in the warm air, but the temptation of her body was too much of an allure for him to give up.

Sliding his hands down her neck to that very knot, he released it, and slowly began to open her towel, letting it drop to the floor in a heap.

She didn't try to hide her body from him, and for that he was thankful. His cock sprang to life, hard, pulsing, demanding, but he ignored it. He was going to take tonight to give Pepper a night she would never forget. This was all about her and the two of them together. He pushed thoughts of her stepfather, responsibility, and Killer of Kings to the back of his mind.

He had tonight, and he was going to make every single moment count.

Stepping away from her body, he removed his shirt, placing his gun on the small cabinet beside the bed, and opened his belt. Piece by piece he became as naked as she was.

Once he wore nothing, he stepped up to her, wrapping his arms around her waist, and pulling her close.

Just the feel of her naked body pressing against his own, Viper was in heaven. In his world, he had more money than he could ever spend, but he had never had the one thing that he had craved as a little boy—love. Until now, Viper had never known what it was like to love a woman, or to be loved by her. Many nights, he would lie on the cold ground, shaking, shivering, and begging for someone to take him away. He craved someone to love him, to hold him close more than anything.

When Pepper wrapped her arms around him, he sighed, contented.

"I wanted you so much, Pepper. When I was a boy, I wanted a woman, and you are my dream come true. There is no one else for me in this world." He pulled back just enough to press a kiss to her lips. "And I will do everything in my power to keep you alive."

****

Pepper didn't know whether to laugh or cry. She had never wanted a man in her life, and had always believed she would be nothing more than a lonely businesswoman, with the family empire to keep her company. Viper exploded onto her scene in more ways than she could have ever imagined. Against all odds, he had saved her when he didn't have to, and she had fallen in love with him.

Maybe it was that Stockholm thing, but then again, Viper had never hurt her. Sure, he'd grabbed her roughly a couple of times, but the moment he saw that he was hurting her, he released his hold. He was entirely the wrong kind of man to love, and yet, the perfect one. He never took crap from anyone, and he was a damn fierce man.

She loved him with all of her heart, and knew that he would take a bullet for her. She didn't want him to though. Sinking her fingers into the short hairs at the back of his nape, she smiled at him, and tried to control the tears that were threatening to fall.

"I love you, Pepper."

They fell. She couldn't contain her tears anymore, and nor did she want to. "Let's go away together, Viper. In time everything will die down, and we can live happily, just the two of us. I don't want my family's empire. I only want you. That's all I want."

He held her close. "They will never stop hunting you, and your stepfather will only get desperate. We have tonight, baby. Give me tonight, and then I will make sure you never have anything else to fear."

She closed her eyes, and then pressed her lips against his. No matter what it took, she would stop him. Pepper would make sure that he didn't go and find hell, but that he stayed, and loved her.

Viper wrapped his large, muscular arms around her, one hand going to the back of her head, holding onto her tightly. She loved how he held her, how his arms helped her to feel comfort. So many had died because of him, but not her. He held her, protected her, and above everything else, he loved her.

His tongue traced her lips, and she opened to him, wanting his kiss, needing him more than anything. Pushing all of her fears to one side, she concentrated on the moment she had with Viper, loving him, being surrounded by him, consumed by him.

Running the tips of her fingers down his back, she marveled at the man in her arms, knowing what it had cost him to open up like that. His body pressed against hers, Pepper was in total heaven. She held her thighs together as heat rushed through her body. She was so wet already, and it was kind of embarrassing. When it came to Viper, he inspired so much inside her that it was next to impossible to keep it contained.

She loved him.

She wanted him.

Their lives were in danger, and he was going to do something crazy, and stupid. She wanted to make him stop, but for now, she just wanted to have this time with him.

Pulling away from the kiss, he pressed her lips against his neck, and then down his shoulder toward his chest. She flicked her tongue against one nipple, and then over to the next. His hand tightened in her hair, and she couldn't help the moan that slipped through her lips. Glancing up, she saw that his gaze was on hers, and there was no mistaking the fire within his eyes.

Slowly, she worked down his body until she was on her knees. His hand still in her hair, only this time, it was wrapped around his fist. Her nipples grew hard, and she stared up the length of his body. His cock, long, thick, and hard, pointed toward her, begging to be licked. The tip was covered in pre-cum. She licked her lips.

"You don't have to do this, babe."

"I want to do this. I want to give you pleasure, Viper. Just you." She wrapped her fingers around his length, and slid her tongue down the vein, closing her eyes.

He groaned, and she covered the tip, taking him into her mouth. She sucked hard on his cock, loving the way he filled her mouth. His pre-cum coated her tongue, and she swallowed it down.

Viper tightened his hold on her hair, and she smiled against him.

Finally opening her eyes, she looked at him, to see the wild man blazing in his eyes.

"Your mouth feels fucking incredible."

She pulled off his cock. "You're the only man

I've ever touched like this. The only one I ever want to suck, to lick, to kiss."

"You're mine, Pepper. No matter what happens, you're fucking mine, and I will always take care of you."

The moment he said the last word, she took most of his cock into her mouth until he hit the back of her throat. She bobbed her head on his cock, relishing the taste of him as more pre-cum leaked into her mouth. She lapped it up, loving the sounds he was making.

This was all hers, and she loved this man.

It was crazy, and completely against everything she had ever known, but she didn't care. She loved Viper, the killer, the man, every single part of him.

He pulled her up by her arms, and slammed his lips down on hers. At the same time, he moved them back until her legs hit the bed, and she dropped down onto the sheets. He didn't release her.

Spreading her thighs, she broke from the kiss to watch as he fisted his cock, running his hand up and down his impressive length. He placed the tip against her slit, and began to thrust so that he bumped her clit.

"You're so wet for me, baby. Tell me what you want."

"I want you, Viper. Fuck me, take me, I'm all yours."

"I've never had a woman that's all mine, and I'm going to take you, possess you, claim you, and fucking own you." He eased his cock down to her entrance, and slammed to the hilt within her. She screamed his name, her nails sinking into his flesh, holding on tightly to him. "You're so tight, so perfect, so fucking mine."

He captured her hands and pressed them beside her head. His lips were on hers, hungrily kissing, biting, and consuming her with his heat.

Viper pulled out of her pussy so that only the tip

was inside her. He didn't give her the chance to get accommodated to his length. Slamming every single inch inside her, he pounded inside her so that the headboard hit the wall.

In one quick move, he flipped them around so that he was lying on the bed, and his hands were on her hips, holding her. "I want you to ride me, baby."

Heat flooded her cheeks. She couldn't do this. Resting her hands on his shoulders, Viper seemed to understand her hesitation, and took control, showing her exactly what he liked.

"So perfect, so beautiful, all mine." He kept on repeating the words that she belonged to him, and she loved hearing it.

She began to rock her hips, lifting herself up, and then thrusting down onto his cock. Viper moved his hands from her tits, going down to her hips, and then running along her thighs, going to her pussy. She looked down, and watched as he spread the lips of her pussy even as he filled her. He started to stroke her clit, and she flung her head back, moaning as he caressed that tiny bundle of nerves. The pleasure was intense, especially as his cock pulsed like a brand within her. He was so big, and he surrounded her. Not a part of her wasn't owned by him.

"I'm so close, babe. I want you to come all over my cock at the same time. I want to fill you with my spunk."

Pepper loved it when he talked dirty. She watched his eyes as he fingered her pussy. He thrust up inside her as she moved with him. The pleasure was intense, and there was no way for her to hold back, nor did she want to. She came, screaming his name, shaking with the power of her orgasm.

Before she had even finished, Viper grabbed her

hips, slammed within her three times, and erupted, his cum spilling inside her. She felt every single pulse as his cock filled her.

Viper pulled her down, kissing her shoulder, and she closed her eyes. The night was young, and he wasn't finished with her, she just knew it.

Chapter Ten

Viper stroked Pepper's back as she cuddled in the crook of his arm. He knew their time together was limited, and it pissed him off that things weren't different. In his perfect world, Pepper would be safe and he'd be everything she needed. But since his reality was fucked up, he'd have to fight for what he wanted—and he would.

"Where will you live when this all settles down?" he asked.

He felt her shrug. "I guess I've always dreamed of a little place by the water. It's so peaceful and relaxing. I've never been a city person."

"Is there room for me in that little place?"

She giggled. "Yes, I need someone to scare away the seagulls."

"I can do that."

Viper was irrevocably in love with Pepper. His nomad lifestyle based on money, death, and keeping numb meant nothing to him now. All he wanted to do was make Pepper's dreams come true.

"Who was that man? The one you didn't kill."

He hadn't told her much about Bain. What was there to tell? He was raised in the same compound as Viper. They'd grown up together, living out the same twisted childhood that would give the strongest person nightmares. Once they all split up as teens, he'd only seen him on a couple rare occasions. Like Viper, he worked as a hired mercenary, but he refused to work for anyone, including Killer of Kings. Bain played it solo, a reclusive and sadistic motherfucker who refused to answer to anyone.

Still, he was the closest thing to a brother Viper had.

"Bain was taken as a boy, the same as me. We both got the short end of the stick when it came to happy childhoods."

"Why would he attack you then?"

Viper chuckled. "You wouldn't understand, baby girl. We were taught to close off our hearts. It was drilled into us every single day. He's probably more animal than man at this point in his life. He's dangerous, unstable. I never want him that close to you ever again."

"If he's so horrible, why didn't you kill him?"

Viper felt a wave of emotion fill his dark soul. "It's not his fault. Those assholes created a monster. They created me." He held her tighter. "You brought out something in me I thought was dead. Maybe there's hope for Bain, too."

They'd been resting together, talking, and sharing for hours. It was the last guaranteed night they had together, so he knew he had to claim Pepper completely. He wanted her to be his in every way. His cock was already raring to go again. Her curves and sweet innocence were a wicked combination for his libido. Opposites really did attract in their case.

He rolled atop her, grinding his cock against her mound. She moaned and ran her hands over his back.

"How can you be horny again?" she asked. "You can't be human."

"I'll never get enough of you, sweet girl." He painted a line along the smooth plane of her neck with his tongue. Then he kissed her, tasting and sampling, knowing exactly what he wanted next. "I need to make you mine."

"I *am* yours. Only yours."

"Not all of you, and I want it all." He nuzzled her neck, nipping on her earlobe.

"What more can I give you?" she asked, tilting

her head aside. Damn, she was adorable. He almost felt guilty for what he was going to take from her. Almost.

"I want your ass. From the first day I saw you, I've wanted that beautiful ass of yours." His cock twitched in anticipation.

Pepper tensed under him. "I don't know, Viper. You're so big. It'll be painful."

He growled just thinking about it. His little virgin had more firsts to give, and he wanted to claim them all. "I'd never hurt you. I only want to make you feel good."

She ran her finger along the bruise around his eye. "I trust you," she said. "But I'm still scared."

Viper loved that she trusted him. He saw it as a responsibility, an honor of sorts. Everyone he dealt with was afraid of him and expected the worst—not Pepper.

"Roll over for me. I'll go slow, so slow you'll be begging me to fuck your ass."

Once she was on her stomach, he straddled her legs and held those huge, luscious globes in his palms. He gave them a little shake, mesmerized by the wiggle, and tempted to give her a bite or two. Viper couldn't resist giving her a little smack, the fleshy sound filling the room. She squealed.

"Fuck, Pepper. You're everything I could want in a woman." He shifted down the bed so he could lean over and kiss her ass. "Get up on your knees for me."

She did as she was told, lifting up onto her hands and knees. He pressed her back down until her cheek rested on the mattress, her ass high in the air, doggy-style. "We should turn the light off in the hall," she said.

"I don't think so. I want to see every minute of this." The soft light from the hallway filtered into the bedroom, allowing him to see her ass and pussy on full display for him. She was ripe and swollen, her folds soft and pink. He'd thought she was over her self-conscious ways. Viper would have to teach her some manners. "If you try to hide yourself from me again, I'll spank you a hell of a lot harder. Do you know how many women pay to have a luscious ass like this? Now, I want you to stay put."

Viper leaned over and kissed her pussy. He used the tip of his tongue to rim her asshole, teasing the sensitive area until Pepper whimpered. The fucking sounds she made slithered through his body, settling in his cock.

He left the room to get a small tube of lube from his toiletry bag in the bathroom. When he returned she hadn't moved, her naked body poised and ready. He smoothed his hand around her ass cheek, feeling her skin break into gooseflesh under his touch. He drizzled the lube on her tight little rosette. She'd be fucking tight, and he couldn't wait to feel her squeeze his cock.

"Viper, I'm scared."

"You want me to stop?"

She shook her head.

He smiled as he kneeled on the edge of the bed. "Relax for me. Going tense will only make this harder. You said you trust me, right?"

"Yes…"

"Okay then. Feel my fingers slide into your ass. Tell me how this feels, sweetheart." He entered her virgin hole with two fully lubed fingers. Every move he made was slow and measured. He had to control his own breathing because he'd never been more anxious to fuck.

She gasped. "It feels so good."

"You have no idea the things I can show you." With his thumb he entered her pussy, teasing her G-spot until the tension melted from her body. He began to slide his fingers almost out, then back in, over and over. The fact she was giving herself to him was a gift he didn't take lightly. Yes, he wanted to own her, but it would be meaningless if he had to take what he wanted. Pepper's submission was perfect, and exactly what he craved most.

Her panting became erratic, and she pushed back against him to get more of his fingers. She was primed, so he began to scissor his fingers, stretching her virgin entrance.

"Think you can handle my dick, baby? I'll go nice and easy." He hoped she didn't back out now because his cock felt like lead, pre-cum slipping from the tip. It was getting painful holding back, every little moan from Pepper making his girth throb to the beat of his heart.

"Yes. I want you inside me, Viper. I love you."

Mine.

He positioned himself behind her, adding an overflow of lube to be safe. Then he grasped her hips, sinking his fingers into her soft flesh. Viper took a few cleansing breaths to remind himself to take it slow when he wanted to fuck her like a damn animal. "Okay, just relax, Pepper." He pressed his tip to her impossibly tight asshole, finding it difficult to gain entrance. "Bear down against my cock and let me fill you. God, you drive me crazy."

"I'm trying," she said.

He didn't quit, knowing things would loosen up once he passed those first few inches. And he had a lot of inches on the way, all for her. He played with her clit the entire time, rolling the little bud in quick circles. As he sank into her rear, his eyes lolled back in his head. It was fucking heaven on Earth.

"Oh God, Viper!"

He needed her to last longer than a few minutes. Fuck, he wished he could hold back all night long and enjoy her until the sun came up. He began to ease out and slide back in, building up a slow, steady rhythm. The light from the hall was just enough so he could watch his cock pump in and out, disappearing deep inside her over and over. The sight alone was enough to make his balls pull up tight, an orgasm dangerously close.

"You're such a good girl, taking my whole cock in your tight little ass. I love fucking you." His body was slick with sweat, his chest heaving.

"I'm going to come, Viper," she cried out. "I'm going to come!" She was on the edge, unsure how to handle all the new sensations. He wanted to be the one to show her everything.

"Let it go, baby. Milk my dick with your ass. Don't hold back."

When she climaxed, she screamed and cried, completely wanton. He filled her with his seed, savoring every second until he was fully spent. Then he collapsed to his back, his arms splayed.

Pepper crawled beside him, leaning over to lick the sweat off his pec. "That was so good. Better than I could have ever imagined."

She was going to be the death of him. He was down for the count, exhausted from fucking all night. "I'm glad," he said. "Come here."

"I've never felt safer than when I'm with you," she said, resting her head on his chest. "I've always been afraid, and I never really belonged."

"You feel safe with a hitman? I was hired to kill you."

She traced his muscles, and he loved the feel of her delicate touch on his body.

"But you didn't."

He used a crooked finger to lift her head. She looked up at him with those big, blue eyes, and he kissed her. This kiss wasn't about sex or passion. Since he couldn't write her flowery words, he'd show her how he felt. He gave her a piece of himself with the kiss.

They fell asleep in each other's arms. It was like his past and all the pain were drowned out by Pepper's sweetness. During these brief moments, he was a normal man, not scarred and damaged.

He woke up with a start, jerking up into a sitting position, his heart racing. How long had he been asleep? He'd had another nightmare. But this one was different. Pepper was out of reach, skirting the edge of a cliff, the ocean waves crashing far below. He beckoned her to come, but there were hired guns moving in on her from the other direction. His fear of heights wasn't even an afterthought, but he was still too late to save her.

Even knowing it was all in his head, Pepper sleeping like an angel beside him, his nerves were on edge. He turned to the side, brushing some stray blonde hairs off her face. She looked even younger when sleeping, pure and beautiful. *His wife.* It might only be printed on a piece of paper, but it meant something. It was a commitment burned into every facet of his being. And he had to make things right. Boss wanted him to use her as bait, but fuck that shit. Viper wouldn't risk her. This was all on him.

Viper quietly slipped away from the warm bed, Pepper's vanilla scent clinging to the sheets. He cleaned up in the bathroom, staring at himself in the foggy mirror. He was going to be thirty-five soon, although he didn't really have a birthday. Everything about his life was fabricated. He didn't exist—he didn't even have fucking fingerprints. Pepper was fifteen years younger, wholesome and full of life, the last type of woman he envisioned for himself. In order to keep her safe, he had to put his happily ever after fantasy on the back burner. Tonight was all about death—death for everyone in his way.

He dressed in black, strapping on as much heat as he could carry. Maybe Bain would prove him wrong and have a fucking heart. He doubted it.

Before he left the hotel, he desperately wanted to write Pepper a good-bye letter in case he didn't come back. He wanted to tell her that her unconditional love had changed him, awakened him. That she was his everything, and he'd do anything for her happiness, even if it meant his own death. Finally, he'd tell her he loved her, needed her, and wanted to be a better man because of her. A week with her was better than a lifetime without her.

Viper turned off the hall light. His life had always been a forfeit. Maybe dying a martyr was the only way to redeem his soul.

****

Pepper stretched and wiggled under the sheets, her body pleasantly sore. She was not expecting anal sex to be so satisfying. Just remembering that wildfire of sensation made her tingle all over, hungry for more. Viper had brought her to a level of pleasure she didn't think was possible. The man was sex on a stick, and all hers.

The early morning sun peeked in through the cracks in the curtains. She wondered where Viper was. Pepper wrapped the top sheet around her body and made her wall to the hallway. "Viper?"

She frowned when he didn't answer. And panicked after searching the entire suite and finding him missing. All she could envision was him dead, and her legs nearly gave out thinking about it. He could have walked away so many times, taken her money, and lived out his life in peace. But he'd stuck around, gave her the love she desperately craved, and promised her protection. And, she hoped, forever.

Now he had some death wish, probably back at her house on a killing spree. But he had no idea how insane her stepfather was. By now, he'd have increased his security, and then there was Bain, a dangerous weakness for Viper.

Why couldn't he have just run away with her? What if she never saw him again? He might be a nightmare to most people, but she knew better. He was the only man to make her feel beautiful and special. He'd taken her virginity, shown her pleasures she never imagined possible. And he was her husband.

Pepper raced to get dressed, dancing into her clothes. She had to do something to stop him. Or was it too late?

The entire time she prayed he was just out getting food. She wanted him to walk through that door, his larger than life presence standing in the foyer.

She remembered the last time she'd gone in search of him, and how badly that had turned out. This time she'd be more cautious. Pepper cracked open the door and peeked outside. There were two huge men in dark suits on sentry duty. She eased the door closed and locked it tight. Her heart pounded, her adrenaline surge making her dizzy. Her stepfather had found her. Had he already killed Viper?

What am I going to do?

They were on the first floor so Pepper rushed around the suite, checking for any other exit. The bedroom window faced a busy street, and she couldn't see any sketchy men lurking around. She needed Viper, needed his strength and confidence right now.

I have to do this myself.

Pepper slid open the window and struggled to get her leg out first. Why couldn't she have cat-like stealth? She ended up falling onto the lawn in a heap, bruising her hip in the process.

As she got to her feet, brushing the dirt off her pants, she noticed a set of shiny black shoes. She held her breath, and looked up.

"Stay away from me," she warned. Pepper eyed the street and then the stranger. If she had to she'd scream or make a break for the road.

"Relax. I'm here to keep an eye on you. Viper's orders."

Her mouth fell open. This hulking guy didn't look friendly, but at least he wasn't there to kill her. She nearly sank in relief. "Who are you?"

"I work for Killer of Kings. That's all you need to know."

She huffed. "Where's Viper?"

"Like he'd tell me."

Pepper crossed her arms over her chest. She couldn't stay here and do nothing. "I'm not your prisoner. I can leave if I want to."

He didn't say anything, and he certainly didn't look intimidated by her threat.

"You realize he's probably off getting himself killed right now? We can't just stay here and do nothing."

The man scoffed. "Trust me, he can take care of himself."

Pepper shook her head. "Not this time. Look, I'm catching a cab, and if you try and stop me I'll scream. I can scream so loud, the entire block will hear."

When she started to march to the street, feigning confidence, he grabbed her arm and held her back.

"Hey!"

"You're not leaving. You can scream all the fuck you want. I'll put you over my shoulder and tie you up if I have to."

She was no match for this brute of a man, but she

loved Viper too much to give up now.

"Can't you do anything? Send back-up? Call him?"

He began to lead to her around the building by the arm, like she was some toddler who'd been up to no good. Her requests were in vain. "When he left last night, he was strapping enough firepower to take out a small army. If anyone needs to worry, it's whoever pissed him off."

This guy's confidence in Viper's ability gave her a measure of reassurance. It was just that she loved him so damn much. The thought of him getting killed or even hurt just to ensure she could live without looking over her shoulder was too much. Tears pricked at her eyes as he escorted her back to her hotel room.

If he'd left in the night, why wasn't he back yet? Pepper had a really bad feeling. She needed to know before she drove herself crazy. She stood in the entrance of her suite. "Can I pay you? How much would it take for you to drive me to my old house? You'd still be babysitting me, so no harm done, right? I just need to check on Viper. I can wire you five grand in two minutes."

He laughed without humor, not falling for her deal, and she noticed gun handles when his suit jacket shifted. The guy's cell rang, and he turned his back to her when he answered it. "No, he's gone, but the girl's here." She could hear angry garbled words coming from the phone. "Boss, you think I could stop him once he had his mind set? He wanted to go alone. Yeah, I still have the stuff. Okay, I'll follow through."

"What's happening?" she asked.

"Viper's gone rogue, so I have to clean up his shit trail, that's what. I'll meet you in the front. Navy SUV. Two minutes. Looks like you're going to get your wish after all."

Both men stormed off, leaving her alone. Pepper hoped these guys from Killer of Kings could be trusted. She needed protection. Her stepfather had killed her mother, murdered a whole news crew, and put a worldwide hit on her head. It was all for greed, and it made her sick. She wanted to forget it all—the wealth, the status, the mansion, and everything else her stepfather was ready to kill for. All she needed was Viper and a simple life far away from all this madness.

When she met the men at the front, one was waiting with the rear passenger door held open like a limo service. She tentatively sat in the leather seat, feeling nervous and uncertain. When they pulled out into the traffic, the guy she'd spoken with turned around in the passenger seat. He had a wicked grin on his face. The next moment he moved so quickly she didn't have time to react. Pepper looked down at her leg where he'd poked her with a needle.

"Have a good sleep," he said.

Then her eyes were too heavy to hold open.

Chapter Eleven

It didn't take him long to get the main building that Pepper owned, and should rightfully be hers, Henshaw Corporation. The building was large, and tall, and it was still night. Crouching down, Viper quickly looked at the building and saw two guys chatting. Sutherland was a fucking waste of space. He couldn't even hire decent men. Even though he'd hired him, it didn't matter. The bastard was so desperate for money, he'd gone far and wide. This was the only way he was going to be able to keep Pepper safe.

This wasn't a suicide mission—at least he hoped it wasn't. He intended to get back home to her, but there was a chance he wouldn't come out of this alive. One week was all he had of utter perfection. She was perfect for him. All of his life he had dreamed of someone like her, believing with all of his heart he'd never get to hold, to cherish, to love. He had gotten everything his heart desired and more, and yet he felt greedy. He wanted more time with her, but he'd gladly die if it meant she got to live a full and long life. It was the first time that he'd not been a selfish bastard, and that in itself was a shock to him. He was more than willing to kill every single person who stepped in his way.

Years of training had brought him to this moment, and he never thought he would be happy to see death, but this was how it was going to be.

Closing his eyes, he pictured Pepper's beautiful smile. The way she looked at him as he was deep inside her would stay with him forever.

It was now or never.

He moved from his wall, crouching down behind the potted plants corporations seemed to love. When the guy moved near him, he pounced, wrapping his arms around his neck, and snapping it, firing his gun on the man opposite, who went down instantly. The two guards were dead, and wouldn't be able to call it in. He was heading for the door when his cell phone started to buzz. At first, he ignored it, and then tensed. What if Pepper had woken up and she was scared? He had to keep her in the hotel room, safe.

Cursing, he moved away from the window, providing himself with enough cover that no one would catch him.

"Hey, baby, what's wrong?" he asked.

"Well I have to say I've been called many things by my men, but baby isn't one of them," Boss said, causing him to curse.

"What the fuck do you want?"

"Unlike you, I have a plan that gets our ass out of there. You on the other hand are going to be dead."

"Look, I don't have time to deal with this shit. What the fuck do you want?" He really didn't understand Boss at times. The man was a ruthless killer, probably more dangerous than the whole group of men he employed. Viper didn't know his story, nor did he wish to. Something in his gut told him that anyone who knew anything about Boss, didn't live long enough to fucking breathe.

"You're hurting my feelings right now. I did tell you the plan, and you think this little war mission you're on is going to save you? You're fucking wrong."

Viper paused. They had a plan, but he didn't agree to it. He refused.

"What did you do?" he asked.

"From the moment you hung up the phone I knew you would go on this shit for nothing plan. I decided to take matters into my own hands. You see, men are loyal to you because of some brotherhood shit, but they're loyal to me because I pay them."

Viper closed his eyes, knowing without a doubt that Boss had his woman. "Where is she?"

"Safe and sound, and believe it or not, she doesn't even have a pulse."

"You fucking asshole. Shit like that is dangerous. I asked you for one thing, one fucking thing."

"And in the process you thought to take away something that earned me a lot of money."

"You don't own me, asshole."

"I know I don't own you, but you see, I invested a lot of time and money in you. I'm not going to allow you to die just because you love some girl. She is pretty, and I would bet money that you'd even make it out alive, but on the chance that you don't, we're about to make a deal."

Viper removed the phone from his ear, and pressed his hands together in anger, wanting nothing more than to smash the device. Instead, he cracked the muscles in his neck, took a deep breath, and placed the phone back against his ear. "I'm listening."

"Excellent. You're going to cease your attack on the building, and wait for us. We have a very dead looking Pepper. We'll go in and deal with this with the minimum casualties possible. When we're in front of Sutherland, I'll personally put a bullet between his eyes. No one, and I mean no one, messes with me, my men, or my money."

"This is not your fucking fight. I don't work for you. I won't deal with you." He heard the sound of a gun cocking.

"Continue that and I swear to God himself that I will put a bullet right between this bitch's eyes, Viper. Push me. I don't give a shit."

"You'll lose your money."

"I don't care. I told you what I want you to do. Now do it, or tonight was the last night you had with her." Boss ended the call, and Viper gritted his teeth.

Fuck!

He wanted to hit something, to hurt someone or something, and right now he could do neither. He was fucked either way. Resting his head against the wall, he closed his eyes, and took several deep breaths, trying to calm himself.

Boss had outmaneuvered him again. Pepper would have done whatever the bastard asked if she thought for a second that it would keep him safe. He was so going to spank her ass when he got his hands on her. Her butt was going to be sore for days, and hold his handprint like a tattoo.

Stupid woman.

First though, he was going to chain Boss up, and fucking hurt him. That asshole didn't have a clue what was coming to him, and Viper was going to make sure he killed him, take his time, make it long and slow, and then he was going to rejoice at putting his head on a spike right outside of Killer of Kings.

Just thinking of all the ways he was going to kill Boss filled Viper with a pleasure that was able to calm the beast inside him.

"You were taught better than that," Bain said.

Opening his eyes, he turned his head to find his friend leaning against the wall. The man was like a fucking ghost.

"I don't know. It got you out to say hello to me."

"Why did you let me live?" Bain asked. "You and I both know that I wouldn't have done that for you."

"I have my reasons. So, how have you been?" Viper asked. He didn't intend to kill Bain; he couldn't. It was the one vow he had made when they had run together. In a twisted kind of way, Bain was his brother and his best friend.

Bain stepped away from the wall. He was bigger than Viper remembered, far deadlier as well. The man was covered in ink. Swirls of patterns and color went up his arms, and he guessed over his body. It was on his hands, and up his neck. He was just covered. "You got tats on your dick as well?"

"You know this is not going to end well for you."

"I've got a problem with the man you're working for," said Viper.

"Then you've got to take that problem through me."

Viper shook his head. "I can't come with you. I'm being Boss's bitch." He burst out laughing. "Me, being someone's bitch. It's not the first time, and I doubt it will be the last."

"I'm not here to laugh at your jokes or play games, Viper."

"I know. It's just kind of surreal. Been thinking about you for a long time, and to see you here, it kind of makes me feel shit, and yeah, I guess I missed your ass, which is fucking crazy, right?"

Bain simply stared at him as if he was a complete stranger, and Viper wasn't going to lie, it hurt.

"I met a girl," said Viper.

"I know."

"So you do pay attention then."

"I'm not in the mood for this, Viper. He wants the girl dead."

"Did you know he can't afford to pay you?" Viper asked.

"I'm aware of his situation, and I also know that with that girl dead, he'll have access to millions. You've gone soft, Viper. I always make sure I get what I want.

With his stepdaughter dead, it'll be my biggest payday yet."

"I wouldn't say I've gone soft. I'm simply in love." He held his hands out. "You know if you take me in, Boss is going to kill my girl."

Bain reached toward him, and Viper had a choice. He could either go with him, or he could fight. If Boss thought for a second that he didn't fight, he may try to kill Pepper. There was no choice.

"This isn't going to be easy, and I'm not going to be coming willingly."

"I figured as much. You were always a hardass, Viper. Never doing what you were told to do."

Viper shrugged. "I guess I have always been a bit of a rebel, and I can't change who I am."

He stared at his friend, seeing several new scars that hadn't been there the last time.

"You don't have to do this."

"Viper, I always do my job, and I never switch sides."

"I love this woman." For a split second he was sure he saw some hesitation, maybe even a sign of guilt.

"Don't you remember, Viper? Love makes you weak. Women are just for fucking, not for losing yourself over."

He gritted his teeth, knowing that it was either kill or be killed with this man. He clenched his hands into fists, ready to fight, ready to take this man out. He was just about to throw the first punch when he heard the sound of squealing tires, and he looked over to see that Boss had finally decided to show his ass. Viper didn't know if he should be happy or not.

Bain grabbed his gun, and raised it up, aiming at them. "What is the fucking meaning of this?"

Boss opened the side of the truck, and waved.

"Ah, Bain, the guy I thought was long dead."

"Nothing is going to kill me, old man. What the fuck are you doing here?" Bain didn't lower his gun, and Viper also had his gun trained on Bain. He didn't want to use it. Fuck, for the second time that week he was fucking conflicted, and he didn't like it. Numbness was so much easier. Bain was the one guy he had promised himself he would never hurt, no matter what. Why did Sutherland have to go to him? Anyone else, and he'd have gladly ended them without a thought, but Bain was different. He was the only person that was alive from his past. Everyone else was dead. He'd killed them, but Bain, he was the only brother he'd ever known.

"I have dealings with your master." The way Boss said "master", everyone just knew it didn't mean anything good. "I have a gift and a bone to pick with him."

"Whatever you've got, dump it here, and I'll deal with it."

Boss tutted, and right before Viper's eyes, he watched the man turn. The cold, hard killer stared right at Bain. "I've got a problem with that." He reached into the van, and pulled Pepper out. He held her by the neck, and even to Viper, she looked dead. There was no life to her. "He wanted her dead of natural causes, guess what? She died of natural causes."

"You don't seem so cut up about this," Bain said.

Viper stared at Pepper, and then turned to Bain without saying a word.

"I'll take her," Bain said.

Boss shook his head. "Not going to happen."

"You're not getting past me, old man."

Boss placed the gun at Pepper's forehead, right between the eyes. "You see, Bain, that's where you're wrong. He wanted her to die of natural causes. The clause in the will states that the owners of this company cannot be assassinated. I will kill her, and make sure your boss doesn't get a single cent of this girl's earnings."

Checkmate.

Viper held still, watching as Boss didn't avert his gaze and Bain just stared, quietly.

"You wouldn't do it."

Boss pressed the barrel of his gun against her leg, and fired.

Viper couldn't believe it, and he watched as the wound bled out. *Holy fuck!* Boss had just shot Pepper, and she hadn't fucking moved. He had heard of drugs that powerful that rendered the person to give the sense that they were dead.

His stomach twisted as he looked up at Boss, who was about to put a bullet through her head. The bastard had no feelings whatsoever.

"Wait," Bain said.

"I'm not some pansy ass boy you're dealing with, Bain. Pick your words wisely. This bitch means nothing to me." Boss threw back his head and laughed. "I'm ten million up. Bitch thought I was going to keep her safe. I've got nothing to stop me killing this girl."

"Come this way," Bain said.

Boss whistled toward him, and if they lived through this, Viper was going to make him pay for calling him over like a dog.

"You fucking shot her."

"I'm getting us out of this shit-fest. You're fucking welcome." Boss held his gun out, and started walking. Picking Pepper up, Viper wanted to care for her leg, but decided against it. His heart was racing, and he carried her toward Bain, ignoring the man he'd asked to keep an eye on her. He should have known never to ask these fuckers.

Cradling Pepper in his arms, he vowed to take care of her, to make sure she lived, and had an amazing life, filled with love and laughter. She would be a wonderful mother, and as he walked behind Boss, following Bain, he made plans, and started to see a possible future with her. He imagined Pepper standing at the kitchen, pulling freshly baked cookies from the oven. There were two children around her feet, a boy with his dark hair, and a girl with long blonde hair like her mother.

As the image played out, Viper didn't allow himself to cut it off. He held onto his woman, knowing that he would do everything in his power to make sure that it came true. When he was a boy being hurt for not killing puppies or a multitude of other horrors, there had come a point when he simply stopped dreaming. At first, most of his time was spent thinking about getting out, of having someone save him. It had been a childish feeling. No one had come for him. The days had blended into weeks, and then into months, and before he knew it, it was years, and there was nothing in him to fight what was being done. Instead of fighting his captors, he'd trained. He'd fought every single battle, taken every single scar with the knowledge that there would be a time he was stronger than they were, and he could take them out.

It wasn't long before his extra hours of training attracted Bain. The other kid who had fought as deadly as he was. They were the only two to survive, at least that was all he knew had made it out.

Right before the killing had started, Bain had come to him, sitting and watching.

"What the fuck you doin'?"

"I'm training."

"There's no way you'll ever win. They're going to kill you, you know. They kill everyone who tries."

"Which is why I'm not going to try. I'm going to succeed." Viper bent down, picking up the weight, lifting it above his head, holding it there, then lowering it. "If you want to spend the rest of your life being their little bitch, be my guest. I'm not. I'm getting out."

"You won't be good for shit. I've heard others talkin'. They don't want killers out there."

"There will always be a place for me."

Pulling out of the memory, he stepped onto the elevator, holding Pepper in his arms.

"Are you sure you can carry her?" Bain asked. "She looks fat."

"Shut your fucking mouth," Viper said.

"Ah, so you're upset."

"He didn't think I'd kill his girl," Boss said. "She was a nuisance, and I want to get paid."

"It's always the bottom line with you, Boss." Bain stared up at the numbers on the elevator passing.

"I've got a question for you, Bain," Viper said.

"What is it?"

"Do you like this Sutherland? Is that why you're being a loyal lapdog?" he asked.

Bain chuckled, and glanced back. "You learned to read yet?"

Viper paused, and stared at the man before him. Bain gave nothing away, and the elevator doors pinged open, revealing a man behind a rather large desk.

"Well I have to say this is a surprise," Pepper's stepfather said, coming out from behind the desk.

Viper wanted nothing more than to kill the bastard, only he was waiting for Bain. Did Boss even know what those words meant?

"So you're the man that's got men tailing me and mine like fucking dogs," Boss said, stepping up.

Out of the corner of his eye Viper saw five men

all with guns poised at them.

"I've learned that when you want something done, you've got to learn to do it yourself. Ah, here she is." Sutherland moved toward him, and Viper watched him, knowing that he'd be the one to smash his pretty little face in.

He tutted.

The bastard fucking tutted. "She's injured. I'm afraid that means it's going to be a lot less. Put her on the sofa. She must weigh a ton."

Viper was going to beat the shit out of this man, no question about that.

"Now, about payment," Sutherland said.

Viper already had a gun in his hand, and aimed it at the first man. The doors that came from the stairs opened, and more men came out. What the fuck was this bastard's deal? How did he manage to manipulate so many people?

He shot as many of them as he could, and when he ran out of bullets, or he couldn't fire fast enough, he started to fight hand to hand.

****

Everything hurt, and especially her thigh. Whatever had been given to her had knocked her the fuck out. There was so much noise, and it was a struggle to move her hands. Pepper fought to open her eyes.

Gunshots rang out, and it was like a haze was drifting down her body, and minute by minute, she was waking up.

Opening her eyes, she would have jerked if she could. Around her men were fighting, including her stepfather. Just the sight of him had her sick to her stomach. She became more aware with every passing second. She was on the sofa in her father's old office. The bastard was in her father's office, in her family's company. Beside her was a coffee table, and on that was a gun and a handful of loose bullets. She couldn't believe a gun had been left right in front of her. Who had done that?

Viper was fighting with two men, and there was a slightly larger man who she believed was Bain who grabbed one of the men, and snapped his neck. Was Bain on their team?

Had she missed so much? Was it the same day? The same night?

She lifted her hand, and no one paid any attention to her. They were all focused on their own killing. Slowly, she used her arms to crawl over toward the table, dropping on the floor as she did. Picking up the gun, she loaded it as she'd seen Viper do, and stared right at Sutherland.

Her stepfather had murdered her mother, sent her on the run, hired people to kill her, put a worldwide hit out on her, and she was done with him. He was a piece of scum, and she didn't want to see him again. Not ever.

She aimed the barrel at his head, focusing on the front sights. This man was a monster, and without blinking an eye, or hesitating, she fired off one single shot.

That one shot had everyone pausing.

Pepper watched as Sutherland dropped to the floor from a single bullet hole between his eyes. She collapsed down, screaming as the pain radiated through her leg. Being shot fucking hurt!

Who the hell shot her?

Chapter Twelve

Everyone froze once Sutherland dropped to the ground. Time stood still. Only the grandfather clock ticking in the corner could be heard. A trail of blood poured down from the fatal gunshot wound. It was surreal. Viper had planned this murder a hundred times in his head with vibrant detail. He had fucking looked forward to it. Even when Boss said he'd deliver the killing shot, Viper knew he'd be the one to do it. Never had he expected this turn of events.

After the initial shock settled, the stepfather's hired muscle bolted out the door like little pussies. Boss, Bain, and Viper all stood in a large circle with their weapons in hand.

"Well, I suppose this changes things," said Boss, as if discussing the weather. One of his men, the bastard from last night, peered in the doorway and cursed when he saw the scene.

"You were supposed to watch her for me!" Viper said as soon as he saw the piece of shit.

He disappeared outside again.

"I guess I'm not getting paid after all." Bain scratched his forehead with the muzzle of his gun.

Viper had wanted to kill everyone, including Boss. Now that Sutherland was dead, a huge weight had lifted off his shoulders. But he still wanted his revenge.

He pulled a paper from his jacket pocket and waved it once in the air. "You know what this is?" he asked. "It's my marriage certificate. Thanks for that, by the way." He winked at Boss. "Now that this asshole is dead, it means you're all standing in *my* office. And right now, I really want all of you to fuck off."

He knew hitting Boss in the pocketbook would be worse than any physical damage he could inflict on him.

And Bain wouldn't see a penny now that his paycheck was pushing daisies.

"See you around, old friend." Bain holstered his gun and stepped over the body on his way out. Viper wondered if he'd ever see Bain again. Part of him wanted to stop him, and the other part was still pissed off he'd sold out. He knew there was still something good inside him or he wouldn't have helped kill Sutherland's men. But you couldn't change a stone-cold assassin like Bain overnight.

"Just you and me, Viper. Things didn't go exactly according to plan, but hey, everything worked out just fine."

"You shot my fucking girl," he shouted.

"I wouldn't have killed her. It was part of the plan. The plan *you* were supposed to follow."

"And now what?" asked Viper, his arms out to the sides, a gun in each hand. He wanted to end Boss right now, but knew it would only make his life more complicated. Killer of Kings had a fucking army of loyal men, and he didn't want more targets on his back.

"New deal."

He narrowed his eyes. Boss was in no position to give ultimatums. "Really. You think you hold the fucking cards here?"

"Always." Boss chuckled. "You're going to give me that ten mil bonus Pepper promised you for keeping her alive. Besides a little flesh wound, she looks alive and well to me. Actually, make it twenty."

"Are you insane? I ain't giving you shit." Viper couldn't believe the size of this guy's balls.

"Wrong, Viper. You'll do it because I'm the man who's going to handle this cleanup. You think your little killing princess wants to deal with police, court dates, detectives at the hospital, and possible jail time? Never mind how this will play out on the company's stocks. Shareholders tend to shy away from murder and mayhem." He strolled around the office, observing the book collection in the floor to ceiling shelves. "Then, of course, there's the Bianchi family. If you want that contract on your head to magically disappear, I'm the only one who can make that happen."

"How do you plan on doing that?"

"A hit for a hit. As long as I get paid, it'll be taken care of. You know the game. Bottom line, we walk away from this on equal terms, no hard feelings."

Viper couldn't let this go, but he also knew there would be no peace for him and Pepper if that hit stayed on his head. His vengeance could cost him everything, so he had to consider his next words wisely. He remembered his training. He was raised to push away all emotion, not just love, but hatred as well. The best killers were numb, cold, and focused.

"Send one of your docs here for Pepper. I want him here yesterday."

"Done." Boss made a quick phone call as he continued to stroll around the room. "Sorry about the injury, darling, but desperate times and all that shit." He winked at Pepper. Then he was gone.

It took everything in Viper not to shoot him in the back. In fact, he envisioned it with perfect clarity. But Boss wasn't out of character. He'd done what he'd set out to do, and Pepper was alive to see another day. Viper was the one who'd changed.

Once they were alone in the office, he dropped his guns on the coffee table and fell to his knees beside the sofa.

"Are you okay, babe?" he asked.

"I've been shot," she said. "I've actually been shot. It hurts so bad."

His precious girl looked like she'd been hit by a truck, her eyes glazed over, skin pale, and blood dripping from her leg. Just remembering those assholes insulting what he considered perfection made him see red. Now that he had her beside him, he felt a sense of peace because he could protect her from anything.

"The doctor's on his way. Boss only uses the very best, and it'll all be off the books." He positioned the decorative pillows on one end of the sofa and eased Pepper to her back. Viper took off his jacket, tossed it aside, and carefully positioned her.

When she whined, he felt her pain like it was his own.

"Be brave for me. I need to get these pants off." Viper managed to get her partially undressed so he could assess the damage. It was a clean hit, and as much as he didn't want to believe it, Boss knew what he was doing when he took the shot. Viper still didn't approve. He balled up the pants and pressed them to the wound, adding pressure.

Pepper looked him in the eyes once they were on the same level. He hadn't realized he'd been avoiding her, but he had. Was it guilt that he hadn't protected her? Was he afraid of her disappointment? He wasn't sure, but the moment he looked into those big, blue eyes everything became better. She pushed back his demons and managed to bring out the best in him.

"I shouldn't have left you alone," he said. The fact had eaten him up ever since he'd gotten that call from Boss. Not being able to save her had killed him inside. "I never should have trusted anyone with your safety but myself."

Fuck, he definitely should have known better. His entire life, he'd learned that the only person he could count on was himself.

"You were trying to save me, to make things right. I know that."

"But look how that went," he said. "I fucked up."

"No, you did it because you love me. I can never hate you for that." She held his hand, squeezing tight. Poor thing. Viper couldn't stop replaying the moment in his head when Boss had shot her. The act had torn through him like a hot knife through butter, creating a physical pain. His own thoughts scared him because he wanted to kill everyone for hurting Pepper, fuck the consequences. Luckily, he'd kept in control or things would have ended up a lot different.

"When I saw you unconscious, for a minute I thought you were dead." He exhaled and kissed the top of her hand. "I can't lose you. Not ever."

She smiled, that sweet smile that he'd never tire of. Pepper was his own personal sunshine. "But it's over now, right? I did it. I killed him."

Viper chuckled. "Yeah, you did. And right between the fucking eyes. You're in the wrong line of work."

"It's karma," Pepper said. "He murdered my mother, took everything away from me. I wanted to kill him, wanted to see him die for what he did."

"Don't talk like that, it doesn't suit you. You're my sweet girl, and I don't want you filled with darkness like me. I wish you didn't have to go through any of this, baby. You don't deserve any of this shit." Her innocence was tainted. She had to live the rest of her life mourning her mother, and had a kill on her hands. He didn't like it. God, he was a fool in love.

"We can't change the past, but one good thing came out of my stepfather."

"What's that?"

"He hired Killer of Kings, and they sent you. If it

wasn't for his greed, I never would have met you, never would have fallen in love."

Viper leaned in to kiss her when a loud bang stole his attention. He was about to reach for his gun but stopped when he couldn't find a threat.

It was the cleaning crew pushing their way in through the doorway with their supplies. Mr. Sutherland was going to disappear permanently, and Boss would make it look legit if the media got involved. The doctor slipped in behind them with his medical bag.

"Who are all these people?" asked Pepper.

"Cleaning crew and your doctor."

Pepper tried to lift her head to see. "Is that woman with them? The one that likes you?"

He smiled. "No, Lola's not on this crew, but even if she was, you wouldn't have to worry. I'm yours, Pepper. All yours. There'll never be another woman for me."

Even with all the commotion in the room, Viper didn't care. He closed the distance between them and took that kiss.

****

Almost two weeks had passed since that crazy day at her stepfather's office. She'd been drugged, kidnapped, and shot in less than twenty-four hours. And the man who took her mother away from her was out of her life forever. No more looking over her shoulder or fighting for what was rightfully hers. After the life she'd live recently, it felt almost unnatural to have peace and justice. She kept expecting something terrible to happen at any minute.

They'd stayed at a hotel the past couple weeks because Pepper didn't want to return home. It wasn't really home. Home was a feeling of unconditional love and belonging. It was wherever Viper was. Still, the nomad lifestyle was slowly getting to her. She'd been on the run for so long before this that she craved roots, safety, and security. One thing was for sure—Viper never left her out of his sight for long.

The doctor said she'd be recovering for months, but he couldn't believe how clean the gunshot had been, missing anything important, only passing through the side of her thick thigh. It could have been so much worse.

"Where are we going?" she repeated.

"I told you it was a surprise. Just relax and enjoy the view." Viper had been driving for hours. She didn't mind the scenery, fields dotted with cattle and rolling hills of wildflowers, but curiosity was driving her crazy.

"Fine."

They finally started to slow down, so she sat up straight and took notice. The surroundings looked vaguely familiar. She could hear sounds of the ocean from the open sunroof, gulls cawing and children laughing. Maybe they were going to spend a day at the beach. Pepper started to feel excited, like a kid at Christmas, because being near the water made her happiest. God knows she needed a break from reality about now. In addition to her recovery, she'd been dealing with lawyers and accountants as her parents' fortune legally transferred over to her. According to the media, her stepfather had run off with a stripper, living off the grid in Sacramento.

Viper came to a stop after driving down a long, winding driveway lined with cedar hedges.

"I think I know this town."

"You should," he said. "It's where we met."

He came around to the passenger side and helped her out. She walked with a limp, but it was only temporary and not very painful at this point. Viper doted over her since the accident, making her recovery as pleasant as possible. Her huge tattooed beast of a man turned out to be a real sweetheart. With his arm wrapped around her, supporting most of her weight, they took their time and walked to the entrance of a cute little bungalow. As soon as they entered the front door, she could see the ocean and beach through the far windows. The house was waterfront.

"Whose house is this?" she asked. It was so warm and cozy, simplistic but homey. There was a lot of natural wood and a country flair. She noticed an oversized chair with a handmade throw resting on the armrest. Pepper could imagine herself sitting there reading for hours as she listened to the waves.

"It's our house," he said.

Pepper frowned and whirled on him, nearly falling over. "What are you talking about?"

He led her to the private rear patio, and helped her sit beside him on a loveseat with plush floral cushions. "I bought it. It's our home." He tilted her chin so they were eye to eye. "I want to make a life with you, Pepper. A real life. One with love and kids and homecooked meals. I'll even smile at the fucking neighbors when I take the garbage out."

Tears streamed down her cheeks. "But you're a hitman. And I'm heiress to a fortune."

"Forget it all. We can start over, you and me. Make a new beginning."

Viper had lived a nightmare childhood. He'd never known love or family. Now she had a chance to give it to him, to build their own future together. She didn't care about money, fame, or status. This was exactly what she needed and wanted, and Viper knew it.

"How'd you do all this?" she asked. Pepper knew all about the reading issue. Finding and buying property would require at least some paperwork.

"My *friend*, Maurice, helped me out. He's a nice guy. Maybe you'll get to meet him one day."

"And Bain? Have you heard from him again?" He had strong feelings for Bain, and she hated that they couldn't reconnect properly. If she had a sibling, she'd want a relationship with them, and the two men were almost like brothers in the past.

He took a deep breath. "No, he might be a lost cause. I don't think anything or anyone can change him. I just hope one day he can find the same happiness I've found."

"I hope so, too," she said.

Viper tucked her against him. The breeze was warm and gentle, the smell of the ocean in the air. "I want to give you everything, but I'll need your help. I've never done this before, never stayed put or lived a life without killing."

"Well, the killing definitely needs to stop, but I don't want to change who you are."

He'd been avoiding her sexually since the accident, terrified he'd hurt her, but she wasn't going to break. Her flesh wound was healing nicely, but her libido kept her up most nights. She knew exactly what Viper was capable of giving her and she needed to connect with him on that intimate level. How could he not feel the same?

"Don't worry, I still have guns. You can never be too safe. Even in this shitty little town."

"Hey, it's a quaint town."

He groaned.

"And I wasn't talking about guns. You know I hate them. I was talking about something else," she said. Did she have to spell it out? Pepper ran her hand up his strong thigh, heading north. When she reached his crotch, she gave him a little squeeze. On contact, his cock began to firm up, filling his jeans with a huge bulge. He grabbed her wrist to stop her.

"Baby, you have to heal. Don't tease me."

Pepper was starting to get a complex. "Are you not attracted to me anymore?"

"Are you kidding me? I've been snapping at everyone lately because all I can think about is fucking you."

"Then stop holding back. I need you, Viper. And I trust you not to hurt me."

He released her hand, so she snaked it up his shirt, loving the feel of his hard muscles. A wave of heat flooding her veins, settling between her legs. She needed him, now more than ever.

"You drive me crazy." He kissed her neck, her cheek, and then found her lips. Viper must have been restraining himself because the kiss was pure passion, hungry and desperate. She closed her eyes and absorbed the desire growing between them.

"I love this house," she whispered against his lips.

"I want to make all your dreams come true, baby."

"You already have," she said.

He stood and scooped her up as if she weighed a hundred pounds. She squealed and wrapped her arms around his neck. His strength was such a turn-on. "Sorry, sweetheart, but I've had blue balls all week. Let's christen this house. You have no idea how much I want your sweet little pussy."

Viper would never be a traditional husband—he had a filthy mouth, a no-holds-barred attitude, and fucked like an animal. Still, Pepper wouldn't trade her bad boy for the world.

The End